MOOD
SWINGS

ALSO BY BILL MOODY

The Evan Horne Series

Solo Hand
Death of a Tenor Man
Sound of the Trumpet
Bird Lives!
Looking for Chet Baker
Shades of Blue
Fade to Blue

Other Titles

Czechmate: The Spy Who Played Jazz
The Man in Red Square

BILL MOODY

MOOD SWINGS

Short Stories

Down & Out Books
3959 Van Dyke Rd, Ste. 265
Lutz, FL 33558
www.DownAndOutBooks.com

Cover design by JT Lindroos

ISBN: 1943402094
ISBN-13: 978-1-943402-09-0

CONTENTS

For my daughter Sarah May

THE RESURRECTION OF BOBO JONES

When Brew finally caught up with him, Manny Klein was inhaling spaghetti in a back booth of Chubby's, adding to his already ample girth and plying a green-eyed blonde called Mary Ann Best with tales of his exploits as New York's premier talent scout. As usual, Manny was exaggerating, but probably not about Rocky King.

"The point is," Manny said, mopping up sauce with a hunk of French bread, "this time, you've gone too far." He popped the bread in his mouth, wiped his three chins with a white napkin tucked in his collar and gazed at Brew Daniels with the incredulous stare of a small child suddenly confronted with a modern sculpture. "You're dead, pal. Rocky's put the word out on you. He thinks you're crazy, and you know what? So do I."

Mary Ann watched as Brew grinned sheepishly and shrugged. Nobody had ever called him crazy. A flake, definitely, but with jazz musicians, that comes with the territory, where eccentric behavior is a byword, the foundation of legends.

Everyone knew about Thelonious Monk keeping his piano in the kitchen and Dizzy Gillespie running for president. And who hadn't heard about Sonny Rollins startling passersby with the wail of his mournful saxophone when he found the Williamsburg Bridge an inspiring place to play after he dropped out of the jazz wars for a couple of years.

Strange perhaps, but these things, Brew reasoned, were essentially harmless examples that merely added another layer to the jazz mystique. With Brew, however, it was another story.

Begun modestly, Brew's escapades gradually gathered momentum and eventually exceeded even the hazy boundaries of acceptable behavior in the jazz world until they threatened to eclipse his considerable skill with a tenor saxophone. Brew had the talent. Nobody denied that. "One of jazz's most promising newcomers," wrote one reviewer after witnessing Brew come out on top in a duel with one of the grizzled veterans of the music.

It was Brew's off stage antics—usually at the expense of his current employer—that got him in trouble, earned him less than the customary two weeks' notice and branded him a "bona fide flake." But however outlandish the prank, Brew always felt fully justified, even if his victim violently disagreed. Brew was selective, but no one, not even Brew himself, knew when or where he would be inspired to strike next. Vocalist Dana McKay, for example, never saw Brew coming until it was too late.

Miss McKay is one of those paradoxes all too common in the music business: a very big star with very little talent, although her legion of fans don't seem to notice. Thanks to the marvels of modern recording technology, top-flight studio orchestras and syrupy background vocals, Dana McKay sounds passable on recordings. Live is another story. She knows it, and the bands that back her up know it. When the musicians who hang out at Chubby's heard that Brew had consented to sub for an ailing friend at the Americana Hotel, smart money said Brew wouldn't last a week, and Dana McKay would be his latest victim. They were right on both counts.

To Brew, the music was bad enough, but what really got to him was the phony sentimentality of her act. Shaking hands with the ringsiders, telling the audience how much they meant to her exactly the same way every night—she could produce tears on cue—naturally inspired Brew.

The third night, he arrived early with a stack of McDonald's hats and unveiled his brainstorm to the band. They didn't need much persuading. Miss McKay had, as usual, done nothing to endear herself to the musicians. She called unnecessary rehearsals, complained to the conductor, and treated everyone as her personal slave. Except for the lady harpist, even the string section went along with Brew's plan.

Timing was essential. On Brew's cue, at precisely the moment Miss McKay was tugging heartstrings with a teary-eyed rendition of one of her hits, the entire band donned the McDonald's hats, stood up, arms spread majestically and sang out, "You deserve a break today."

Miss McKay never knew what hit her when the thunderous chorus struck. One of the straps of her gown snapped and almost exposed more of her than planned. She nearly fell off the stage. The dinner show audience howled with delight, thinking it was part of the show. It got a mention in one of the columns, but Dana McKay was not amused.

It took several minutes for the laughter to die down, and by that time, she'd regained enough composure to smile mechanically and turn to the band. "How about these guys. Aren't they some-hing?" Her eyes locked on Brew, grinning inno-cently in the middle of the sax section. She fixed him with an icy glare, and Brew was fired before the midnight show. He was never sure how she knew he was responsible, but he guessed the lady harpist had a hand in it.

Brew kept a low profile after that, basking in the glory of his most ambitious project to date. He made ends meet with a string of club dates in the Village and the occasional wedding. It wasn't until he went on the road with Rocky King that he struck again. Everyone agreed Brew was justified this time, but for once, he picked on the wrong man.

Rocky King is arguably the most hated bandleader in America, despite his nationwide popularity. Musicians refer to him as "a legend in his own mind." He pays only minimum scale, delights in belittling his musicians on the stand and has been known on occasion to physically assault anyone who doesn't measure up to his often unrealistic expectations, a man to be reckoned with. So, when the news got out, King swore a vendetta against Brew that even Manny Klein couldn't diffuse, even though it was Manny who got Brew the gig.

"C'mon, Manny, Rocky had it coming."

Manny shook his head. "You hear that, Mary Ann? I get him the best job he's ever had, lay my own reputation on the line and all he can say is that Rocky had it coming. Less than a week with the band and he starts a mutiny and puts Rocky King off his own bus forty miles from Indianapolis. You know what your problem is, Brew? Priorities. Your priorities are all wrong."

Brew stifled a yawn and smiled again at Mary Ann. "Priorities?"

"Exactly. Now take Mary Ann here. Her priorities are in precisely the right place."

Brew grinned. "They certainly are."

Mary Ann blushed, but Brew caught a flicker of interest in her green eyes. So did Manny.

"I'm warning you, Mary Ann. This is a dangerous man, bent on self-destruction. Don't be misled by that angelic face." Manny took out an evil-looking cigar, lit it and puffed on it furiously until the booth was enveloped in a cloud of smoke.

"Did you really do that? Put Mr. King off his own bus?"

Brew shrugged and flicked a glance at Manny. "Not exactly the way Manny tells it. As usual, he's left out a few minor details." Brew leaned across the table closer toward Mary Ann. "One of the trumpet players had quit, see. His wife was having a baby, and he wanted to get home in time. But kind, generous Rocky King wouldn't let him ride on the bus even though we had to pass right through his hometown. So, when we stopped for gas, I managed to lock Rocky in the men's room and told the driver that Rocky would be joining us later. It seemed like the right thing to do at the time."

"And what has it got you?" Manny asked, emerging from the cloud of smoke, annoyed to see Mary Ann was laughing. "Nothing but your first and last check, minus of course, Rocky's taxi fare to Indianapolis. You're untouchable now. You'll be lucky to get a wedding at Roseland."

Brew shuddered. Roseland was the massive ballroom under the Musician's Union and the site of a Wednesday afternoon nightmare known as cattle call. Hundreds of musicians jam the ballroom as casual contractors call for one instrument at a time. "I need a piano for Saturday night." Fifty pianists or drummers or whatever are called for and rush the stage. First one there gets the gig.

"Did the trumpet player get home in time?" Mary Ann asked.

"What? Oh, yeah. It was a boy."

"Well, I think it was a nice thing to do." Mary Ann leaned back and looked challengingly at Manny.

"Okay, okay," Manny said, accepting defeat. "So, you're the Good Samaritan, but you're still out of work, and I..." He paused for a moment, his face creasing into a smile. "There is one thing. Naw, you wouldn't be interested."

"C'mon, Manny. I'm interested. Anything's better than Roseland."

Manny nodded. "I don't know if it's still going, but I hear they were looking for a tenor player at the Final Bar."

Brew groaned and slumped back against the seat.

"The Final Bar is a toilet. A lot of people don't even know it's still there."

"Exactly," said Manny. "The ideal place for you at the moment." He blew another cloud of smoke and studied the end of his cigar. "Bobo Jones is there with a trio."

"Bobo Jones? *The* Bobo Jones?"

"The same, but don't get excited. We both know Bobo hasn't played a note worth listening to in years. A guy named Rollo runs the place. I'll give him a call if you think you can cut it. Sorry, sport, that's the best I can do."

"Yeah, do that," Brew said in a daze, but something about Manny's smile told Brew he'd be sorry. He was vaguely aware of Mary Ann asking for directions as he made his way out of Chubby's.

It had finally come to this. The Final Bar. He couldn't imagine Bobo Jones there.

The winos had begun to sing.

Brew watched them from across the aisle. Two lost souls, arms draped around one another, wine dribbling down their chins as they happily crooned off-key between belts from a bottle in a paper bag. Except for an immense black woman, Brew and the winos were alone as the 2nd Avenue subway hurtled toward the Village.

"This city ain't fit to live in no more," the woman shouted over the roar of the train. She had a shopping bag wedged between her knees and scowled at the winos.

Brew nodded in agreement and glanced at the

ceiling where somebody had spray painted "*Puerto Rico Independencia!*" in jagged red letters. Priorities, Manny had said. For once, maybe he was right. Even one-nighters with Rocky King were better than the Final Bar.

The winos finally passed out after 42nd Street, but a wiry Latino kid in a leather jacket swaggered on to the car and instantly eyed Brew's horn. Brew figured him for a terrorist, or at least a mugger. It was going to be his horn or the black lady's shopping bag.

Brew picked up his horn and hugged it protectively to his chest, then gave the kid his best glare. Even with his height, there was little about Brew to inspire fear. Shaggy blond curls over a choirboy face and deep-set blue eyes didn't worry the Puerto Rican kid, who Brew figured probably had an eleven-inch blade under his jacket.

They had a staring contest until 14th Street when Brew's plan became clear. He waited until the last possible second, then shot off the train like a firing squad was at his back. He paused just long enough on the platform to smile at the kid staring at him through the doors as the train pulled away.

"Faggot!" the kid yelled. Brew turned and sprinted up the steps, wondering why people thought it was so much fun to live in New York City.

Outside, he turned up his collar against the frosty air and plunged into the mass of humanity that often makes the city look like an evacuation. He elbowed his way across the street, splashing through gray piles of slush that clung to the curbs, soaked shoes and provided cabbies with opportunities to practice their favorite winter pastime of splattering pedestrians. He turned off 7th Avenue, long legs eating up the slippery sidewalk and tried again to envision Bobo Jones playing at the Final Bar, but it was impossible.

For as long as he could remember, Bobo Jones had been one of the legendary figures of jazz piano. Bud Powell, Thelonious Monk, Oscar Peterson— hell, Bobo was a jazz piano giant. But Bobo's career, if brilliant, had also been stormy, laced with bizarre incidents, culminating one night at the Village Vanguard during a live recording session. Before a horrified opening night audience, Bobo had attacked and nearly killed his saxophone player.

Midway through the first set, the crazed Bobo had leapt wild-eyed from the piano, screamed something unintelligible and pounced on the unsuspecting saxophonist, who thought he had at least two more choruses to play. Bobo wrestled him to the floor and all but strangled him with the microphone cord. The saxophonist was already gagging on his mouthpiece and, in the end, suffered enough throat damage to cause him to switch to guitar. He eventually quit music altogether and went into business with his brother-in-law selling insurance in New Jersey.

Juice Wilson, Bobo's two hundred and forty pound drummer, had never moved so fast in his life, unless it was the time he'd mistakenly wandered into a Ku Klux Klan meeting in his native Alabama. Juice dove over the drums, sending one of his cymbals flying into a ringside table of Rotarians. He managed to pull Bobo off the gasping saxophonist with the help of two cops who hated jazz anyway. A waiter called the paramedics, and the saxophonist was given emergency treatment under the piano while the audience looked on in stunned disbelief.

One member of the audience was a photographer for *Time* showing his out-of-town girlfriend the sights of New York. He knew a scoop when he saw it; he whipped out his camera and snapped off a dozen quick ones while Juice and the cops tried to subdue Bobo. The following week's issue ran a photo of Bobo, glassy-eyed, in a straitjacket, with the caption: "Is this the end of Jazz?" The two cops hoped so because they were in the photo too, and their watch commander wanted to know what the hell they were doing in a jazz club if they hadn't busted any dopers.

The critics in the audience shook their heads and claimed they'd seen it coming for a long time as Bobo was taken away. Fans and friends alike mourned the passing of a great talent, but everyone was sure Bobo would recover. He never did.

Bobo spent three months in Bellevue, playing silent chords on the wall of his padded cell and confounding his doctors, who could find nothing wrong; naturally, they diagnosed him as manic depressive and put Bobo back on the street. With all the other loonies in New York, one more wouldn't make any difference.

Bobo disappeared for nearly a year after that. No one knew or cared how he survived. Most people assumed he was living on record royalties from the dozen or so albums he'd left as a legacy to his many fans. But then, he mysteriously reappeared. There were rumors of a comeback. Devoted fans sought him out in obscure clubs, patiently waiting for the old magic to return. But it seemed gone forever. Gradually, all but the most devout drifted away, until, if the cardboard sign in the window could be believed, Bobo Jones was condemned at last to the Final Bar.

Brew knew that much of the story. If he'd known the why of Bobo's downfall, he would have gone straight back to the subway, looked up the Puerto Rican kid and given him his horn. That would have been easier. Instead, he sidestepped a turned-over garbage can and pushed through the door of the Final Bar.

A gust of warm air, reeking of stale smoke and warm beer, washed over him. Dark, dirty and foul smelling, the Final Bar is every Hollywood screenwriter's idea of a Greenwich Village jazz club. To musicians, it means a tiny, poorly lit bandstand, an ancient upright piano with broken keys and never more than a half dozen customers, if you count the bartender.

Musicians play at the Final Bar in desperation, on the way up. For Bobo Jones, and now perhaps Brew Daniels as well, the Final Bar is the last stop on the downward spiral to oblivion. But there he was, one of the true legends of jazz. One glance told Brew all he needed to know. Bobo was down, way down.

He sat slumped at the piano, head bent, nearly

touching the keyboard, and played like a man trying to recall how he used to sound. Lost in the past, his head would occasionally jerk up in response to some dimly remembered phrase that just as quickly snuffed out. His fingers flew over the keys frantically in pursuit of lost magic. A forgotten cigarette burned on top of the piano next to an empty glass.

To Bobo's right were bassist Deacon Hayes and drummer Juice Wilson, implacable sentinels guarding some now forgotten treasure. They brought to mind a black Laurel and Hardy. Deacon, rail-thin and solemn-faced, occasionally arched an eyebrow. Juice, dwarfing his drums, stared ahead blankly and languidly stroked his cymbals in slow, sweeping circles. They had remained loyal to the end and this was probably it.

Brew was mesmerized by the scene. He watched and listened and slowly shook his head in disbelief. A knife of fear crept into his gut. He recognized with sudden awareness the clear, unmistakable qualities of despair and failure that hovered around the bandstand like a thick fog.

Brew wanted to run. He'd seen enough. Manny's message was clear, but now a wave of anger swept over him, forcing him to stay. He spun around toward the bar and saw what could only be Rollo draped over a barstool. A skinny black man in a beret, chin in hand, staring vacantly at the hapless trio.

"You Rollo? I'm Brew Daniels." Rollo's only response was to cross his legs. "Manny Klein call you?"

Rollo moved only his eyes, inspected Brew, found him wanting and shifted his eyes back to the bandstand. "You the tenor player?" he asked contemptuously.

"Who were you expecting, Stan Getz?" Brew shot back. He wanted to leave, just forget the whole thing. He didn't belong here, but he had to prove it. To Manny and to himself.

"You ain't funny, man," Rollo said. "Check with Juice."

Brew nodded and turned back to the bandstand. The music had stopped, but Brew had no idea what they had played. They probably didn't know either, he thought. What difference did it make? He tugged at Juice's left arm that dangled near the floor.

"Okay if I play a couple?"

Juice squinted at Brew suspiciously, took in his horn case, and gave a shrug that Brew took as reluctant permission. He unzipped the leather bag and took out a gleaming tenor saxophone.

He knew why Manny had sent him down here. There was no gig. This was a lesson in humility. It would be like blowing in a graveyard. He put the horn together and blew a couple of tentative phrases. "'Green Dolphin Street' okay?"

Bobo looked up from the piano and stared at Brew like he was a bug on a windshield. "Whozat?" he asked, pointing a long slim finger. His voice was a gravelly whisper, like Louis Armstrong with a cold.

"I think he's a sax man," Juice replied defiantly. "He's gonna play one." Bobo had already lost interest.

Brew glared at Juice. He was mad now, and in a hurry. Deacon's eyebrows arched as Brew snapped his fingers for the tempo. Then Brew was off, on the run from despair.

Knees bent, chest heaving, body rocking slightly, Brew tore into the melody and ripped it apart. The horn, jutting out of his mouth like another limb, spewed fire. Harsh abrasive tones of anger and frustration that washed over the unsuspecting patrons—there were five tonight—like napalm, grabbing them by the throat and saying, "Listen to this, dammit."

At the bar, Rollo gulped and nearly fell off the stool. In spite of occasional lapses in judgment, Rollo liked to think of himself as an informed jazz critic. He'd never fully recovered from his Ornette Coleman blunder. For seventeen straight nights, he'd sat sphinx-like at the Five Spot, watching the black man with the white plastic saxophone before finally declaring, "Nothin', baby. Ornette ain't playing nothing." But this time, there was no mistake. In a bursting flash of recognition, Rollo knew.

Brew had taken everybody by surprise. Deacon's eyebrows were shooting up and down like windshield wipers on high. Juice crouched behind the drums and slashed at the cymbals like a fencer. They heard it too. They knew.

Brew played like a backup quarterback in the final two minutes of the last game of the year with his team behind seventeen to nothing. He ripped off jagged chunks of sound and slung them about the Final Bar, leaving Juice and Deacon to scurry after him in desperate pursuit. During his last scorching chorus, he pointed the bell of his horn at Bobo, prodding, challenging, until he at last backed away.

Bobo reacted like a man under siege. He'd begun as always, staring at the keyboard as if it were a giant puzzle he'd forgotten how to solve. But by Brew's third chorus, he seized the lifeline offered and struggled to pull himself out of the past. Eyes closed, head thrown back, his fingers flew over the keys, producing a barrage of notes that nearly matched Brew's.

Deacon and Juice exchanged glances. Where had they heard this before?

Rollo, off the stool now, rocked and grinned in pure joy. "Shee-it," he yelled.

Bobo was back.

By the end of the first week, word had gotten around. Something was happening at the Final Bar, and people were dropping in to see if the rumors were true. Bobo Jones had climbed out of his shell and was not only playing again, but presenting a reasonable facsimile of his former talent, inspired apparently by a fiery young tenor saxophonist. It didn't matter that Brew had been on the scene for some time. He was ironically being heralded as a new discovery. But even that didn't bother Brew. He was relaxed.

The music and his life were, at least for the moment, under control. Mary Ann was a regular at the club—she hadn't signed with Manny after all—

and by the end of the month, they were sharing her tiny Westside apartment.

But gnawing around the edges were the strange looks Brew caught from Deacon and Juice. They'd look away quickly and mumble to themselves while Rollo showed Brew only the utmost respect. Bobo was the enigma, either remaining totally aloof or smothering Brew with attentive concern, following him around the club like a shadow. If Brew found it stifling or even creepy, he wisely wrote it off as the pianist's awkward attempt at gratitude and reminded himself that Bobo had spent three months in a mental ward.

Of his playing, however, there was no doubt. For some unknown reason, Brew's horn had unlocked Bobo's past, unleashing the old magic that flew off Bobo's fingers with nightly improvement. Brew himself was a big beneficiary of Bobo's resurgence as his own playing reached new heights. His potential was at last being realized. He was loose, making it with a good gig, a good woman. Life had never been sweeter. Naturally, that's when the trouble began.

He and Mary Ann were curled up watching a late movie when Brew heard the buzzer. Opening the door, Brew found Bobo standing in the hall, half hidden in a topcoat several sizes too big, and holding a stack of records under his arm.

"Got something for you to hear, man," Bobo rasped, walking right past Brew to look for the stereo.

"Hey, Bobo, you know what time it is?"

"Yeah, it's twenty after four." Bobo was

crouched in front of the stereo, looking through the records.

Brew nodded and shut the door. "That's what I thought you'd say." He went into the bedroom. Mary Ann was sitting up in bed.

"Who is it?"

"Bobo," Brew said, grabbing his robe. "He's got some music he wants me to hear. I gotta humor him I guess."

"Does he know what time it is?"

"Yeah, twenty after four."

Mary Ann looked at him quizzically. "I'll make some coffee," she said, slipping out of bed.

Brew sighed and went back to the living room. Bobo had one of the records on the turntable and was kneeling with his head up against the speaker. Brew recognized it as one of his early recordings with a tenor player named Lee Evans, a name only vaguely familiar to Brew.

Brew studiously avoided the trap of listening to other tenor players, except maybe John Coltrane. No tenor player could avoid Coltrane, but Brew's style and sound were forged largely on his own. A mixture of hard brittle fluidness on up-tempos balanced by an effortless shifting of gears for lyrical ballads—a cross between Sonny Rollins and Stan Getz. Still, there was something familiar about this record, something he couldn't quite place.

"I want to do this tune tonight," Bobo said, turning his eyes to Brew. It was the first time Bobo had made any direct reference to the music since they'd started playing together.

Brew nodded, absorbed in the music. What was

it? He focused on the tenor player and only vaguely remembered Mary coming in with coffee. Much later, the record was still playing and Mary Ann was curled up in a ball on the couch. Early morning sun streamed in the window. Bobo was gone.

"You know, it's funny," Brew told Mary Ann later. "I kind of sound like that tenor player Lee Evans."

"What happened to him?"

"I don't know. He played with Bobo quite a while, but I think he was killed in a car accident. I'll ask Rollo. Maybe he knows."

But if Rollo knew, he wasn't saying. Neither were Juice or Deacon. Brew avoided asking Bobo, sensing it was somehow a taboo subject, but it was clear they all knew something he didn't. It became an obsession for Brew to find out what.

He nearly wore out the records Bobo had left, and unconsciously, more and more of Lee Evans' style crept into his own playing. It seemed to please Bobo and brought approving nods from Juice and Deacon. As far as Brew could remember, he had never heard of Lee Evans until the night Bobo had brought him the records. Finally, he could stand it no longer and pressed Rollo. He had to know.

"Man, why you wanna mess things up for now?" Rollo asked, avoiding Brew's eyes. "Bobo's playin', the club's busy, and you gettin' famous."

"C'mon, Rollo. I only asked about Lee Evans. What's the big secret?" Brew was puzzled by the outburst from the normally docile Rollo and became even more intrigued. However tenuous

Bobo's return to reality, Brew couldn't see the connection. Not yet.

"Aw shit," Rollo said, slamming down a bar rag. "You best see Razor."

"Who the hell is Razor?"

"One of the players, man. Got hisself some ladies, and he's...well, you talk to him if you want."

"I want," Brew said, more puzzled than ever.

Mary Ann was not so sure. "You may not like what you find," she warned. Her words were like a prophecy.

Brew found Razor off 10th Avenue.

A massive maroon Buick idled at the curb. Nearby, Razor, in an ankle length fur coat and matching hat, peered at one of his "ladies" from behind dark glasses. But what really got Brew's attention was the dog. Sitting majestically at Razor's heel, sinewy neck encased in a silver stud collar, was the biggest, most vicious looking Doberman Brew had ever seen. About then, Brew wanted to forget the whole thing, but he was frozen to the spot as Razor's dog—he hoped it was Razor's dog—bared his teeth, growled throatily and locked his dark eyes on Brew.

Razor's lady, in white plastic boots, miniskirt and a pink ski jacket, cowered against a building. Tears streamed down her face, smearing garish makeup. Her eyes were riveted on the black man as he fondled a pearl-handled straight razor.

"Lookee here, mama, you makin' ole Razor mad with all this talk about you leavin', and you know what happens when Razor get mad, right?"

The girl nodded slowly as he opened and closed the razor several times before finally dropping it in his pocket. "All right then," Razor said. "Git on outta here." The girl glanced briefly at Brew and then scurried away.

"Whatcha you look at, honky?" Razor asked, turning his attention to Brew. Several people passed by them, looking straight ahead as if they didn't exist.

Brew's throat was dry. He could hardly get the words out. "Ah, I'm Brew Daniels. I play with Bobo at the Final Bar. Rollo said—"

"Bobo? Shee-it." Razor slapped his leg and laughed, throwing his head back. "Yeah, I hear that sucker's playing again." He took off his glasses and studied Brew closely. "And you the cat that jarred them old bones? Man, you don't even look like a musician."

The Doberman cocked his head and looked at Razor as if that might be a signal to eat Brew. "Be cool, Honey," Razor said, stroking the big dog's sleek head. "Well you must play, man. C'mon, it's gettin' cold talkin' to these bitches out here. I know what you want." He opened the door of the Buick. "C'mon, Honey, we goin' for a ride."

Brew sat rigidly in the front seat trying to decide who scared him more, Razor or the dog. He could feel Honey's warm breath on the back of his neck. "Nice dog you have, Mr. Razor." Honey only growled. Razor didn't speak until they pulled up near Riverside Park.

He threw open the door, and Honey scrambled

out. "Go on, Honey, git one of them suckers." Honey barked and bounded away in pursuit of a pair of unsuspecting Cocker Spaniels.

Razor took out cigarettes from a platinum case, lit two with a gold lighter, and handed one to Brew. "It was about three years ago," Razor began. "Bobo was hot, and he had this bad-assed tenor player called Lee Evans. They was really tight. Lee was just a kid, but Bobo took care of him like he was his daddy. Anyway, they was giggin' in Detroit or someplace, just before they was spozed to open here. But Lee, man, he had him some action that he wanted to check out on the way, so he drove on alone. He got loaded at this chick's pad, then tried to drive all night to make the gig." Razor took a deep drag on his cigarette. "Went to sleep. His car went right off the pike into a gas station. Boom! That was it."

Razor fell silent. Brew swallowed as the pieces began to fall into place.

"Well, they didn't tell Bobo what happened 'til an hour before the gig, and them jive-ass dumb record dudes said, seein' how they'd already given Bobo front money, he had to do the session. They got another dude on tenor. He was bad, but he wasn't Lee Evans. At first, Bobo was cool, like he didn't know what was happening. Then, all of a sudden, he jumped on this cat, scared his ass good, screaming, 'You ain't Lee, you ain't Lee.'" Razor shook his head and flipped his cigarette out the window.

Brew closed his eyes. It was so quiet in the car that Brew was sure he could hear his own heart beating as everything came together. All the pieces fell into place except one, but he had to ask. "What's this all got to do with me?"

Razor turned to him, puzzled. "Man, you is one dumb honky. Don't you see, man? To Bobo, you is Lee Evans all over again. Must be how you blow."

"But I'm not," Brew protested, feeling panic rise in him. "Somebody's got to tell him I'm not Lee Evans."

Razor's eyes narrowed; his voice lowered menacingly. "Ain't nobody got to tell nobody shit. Bobo was sick for a long time. If he's playin' again 'cause of you, that's enough. You," he pointed a finger at Brew, "jus' be cool and blow your horn." There was no mistake. It was an order.

"But..."

"But nothin'. If there's anything else goin' down, I'll hear about it. Who do you think took care of Bobo? You know my name, man? Jones. Razor Jones." He smiled at Brew suddenly, seeing that Brew failed to make the connection. "Bobo's my brother."

Razor started the car and whistled for Honey. Brew got out slowly and stood at the curb like a survivor of the holocaust. The huge Doberman galloped back obediently, sniffed at Brew and jumped in next to Razor.

"Bye," Razor called, flashing Brew a toothy smile. Brew could swear Honey sneered at him as the car pulled away.

* * *

The Final Bar was now the "in" place in the Village. Manny had seen to that, forgiving Brew for all his past sins and recognizing Bobo's return, if artfully managed, would ensure all their futures. If anything, Manny was pragmatic. He was on the phone daily, negotiating with record companies and spreading the word that a great event in jazz was about to take place.

Driven by the memory of Razor's menacing smile, Brew played like a man possessed, astonishing musicians who came in to hear for themselves. He was getting calls from people he'd never heard of, offering record dates, road tours, even to form his own group. But of course, Brew wasn't going anywhere. He was miserable.

"You were great, kid," Manny said, looking around the club. It was packed every night now, and Rollo had hired extra help to handle the increase in business. "Listen, wait till you hear the deal I've made with Newport Records. A live session, right here. The return of Bobo Jones. Of course, I insisted on top billing for you, too." Manny was beaming. "How about that, eh?"

"I think I'll go to Paris," Brew said, staring vacantly.

"Paris?" Manny turned to Mary Ann. "What's he talking about?"

Mary Ann shrugged. "He's got this crazy idea about Bobo."

"What idea, Brew? Talk to me."

"I mean," Brew said evenly, "there isn't going to be any recording session, not with me anyway."

Manny's face fell. "No recording? Whatta you

mean? An album with Bobo will make you. At the risk of sounding like an agent, this is your big break."

"Manny, you don't understand. Bobo thinks I'm Lee Evans. Don't you see?"

"No, I don't see," Manny said glaring at Brew. "I don't care if he thinks you're Jesus Christ with a saxophone. We're talking major bucks here. Big. You blow this one and you might as well sell your horn." Manny turned back to Mary Ann. "For God's sake, talk some sense into him."

Mary Ann shrugged. "He's afraid Bobo will flip out again, and he's worried about Bobo's brother."

"Yeah, Manny, you would be too if you saw him. He's got the biggest razor I've ever seen. And if that isn't enough, he's got a killer dog that would just love to tear me to pieces."

"What did you do to him? You're not up to your old tricks again are you?"

"No, no, nothing. He just told me, *ordered* me, to keep playing with Bobo."

"So, what's the problem?"

Brew sighed. "For one thing, I don't like being a ghost. And what if Bobo attacks me like the last time. He almost killed that guy. Bobo needs to be told, but no one will do it, and I can't do it. So, it's Bobo, Razor, or Paris. I'll take Paris. I heard there's a good jazz scene there."

Manny stared dumbly at Mary Ann. "Is he serious? C'mon, Brew, that's ridiculous. Look, Newport wants to set this up for next Monday night, and I'm warning you, screw this up, and I will personally see that you never work again." He laughed and slapped Brew on the back. "Trust me, Brew. It'll be fine."

But Brew didn't trust anyone, and no one could convince him. Even Mary Ann couldn't get through to him. Finally, he decided to get some expert advice. He checked with Bellevue but was told that the case couldn't be discussed unless he was a relative. He even tracked down the saxophonist Bobo had attacked, but as soon as he mentioned Bobo's name, the guy slammed down the phone.

In desperation, Brew remembered a guy he'd met at one of the clubs. A jazz buff, Ted Fisher, was doing his internship in psychiatry at Columbia Medical School. Musicians called him Doctor Deep. Brew telephoned him, explained what he wanted, and they agreed to meet at Chubby's.

"What is this, a gay bar?" Ted Fisher asked, looking around the crowded bar.

"No, Ted, there just aren't a lot of lady musicians. Now look, I—"

"Hey, isn't that Gerry Mulligan over there at the bar?"

"Ted, c'mon. This is serious."

"Sorry, Brew. Well, from what you've told me already, as I understand it, your concern is that Bobo thinks you're his former saxophonist, right?"

Brew looked desperate. "I don't think it, I know it. Look, Bobo attacked the substitute horn player. What I want to know is what happens if the same conditions are repeated. Bobo is convinced I'm Lee Evans now, but what if the live recording session triggers his memory and brings it all back and he suddenly realizes I'm not? Could he flip out again and go for me?" Brew sat back and rubbed his throat.

"Hummm," Ted murmured and gazed at the ceiling. "No, I wouldn't think so. Bobo's fixation, brought about by the loss of a close friend, whom he'd actually, though inadvertently, assumed a father figure role for, is understandable and quite plausible. As for a repeated occurrence, even in simulated identical circumstances, well-delayed shock would account for the first instance, but no, I don't think it's within the realm of possibility." Ted smiled at Brew reassuringly and lit his pipe.

"Could you put that in a little plainer terms?"

"No, I don't think it would happen again."

"You're sure?" Brew was already feeling better.

"Yes, absolutely. Unless..."

Brew's head snapped up. "Unless what?"

"Unless this Bobo fellow suddenly decided he...he didn't like the way you played. Brew? You okay? You look a little pale."

Brew leaned forward on the table and covered his face with his hands. "Thanks, Ted," he whispered.

Ted smiled. "Anytime, Brew. Don't mention it. Hey, do you think Gerry Mulligan would mind if I asked him for his autograph?"

In the end, Brew finally decided to do the session. It wasn't Manny's threats or insistence. They had paled in comparison to Razor. It wasn't even Mary Ann's reasoning. She was convinced Bobo was totally insane. No, in the end, it was the dreams that did it. Always the dreams.

A giant Doberman wearing sunglasses and carrying a straight razor in its mouth was chasing Brew through Central Park. In the distance, Razor stood holding Brew's horn, laughing. Brew had little choice.

On one point, however, Brew stood firm. The Newport Record executives had taken one look at the Final Bar and almost cancelled the whole deal. They wanted to move the session to the Village Vanguard, but Brew figured that was tempting fate too much. Through Mary Ann, Bobo had deferred the final decision to Brew, and as far as he was concerned, it was the Final Bar or nothing. The Newport people eventually conceded and set about refurbishing the broken down club. Brew had to admit, they had really spent some money. The club was completely transformed, with repainting, new tables and chairs, blow up photos of jazz greats on the walls and the sawdust floors replaced with new carpeting.

When Brew and Mary Ann arrived, Rollo, nattily attired in a tuxedo, collecting hefty admission charges and looking as smart as any midtown maître d', greeted them at the door.

"My man, Brew," he smiled, slapping Brew's palm. "Tonight's the night."

"Yeah, tonight's the night," Brew mumbled as they pushed through the crowd of fans, reporters, and photographers. Manny waved to them from the bar where he was huddled with the Newport people. A Steinway grand had replaced the battered upright piano, and a tuner was making final adjustments as engineers scurried about running cables and testing microphones.

Brew suddenly felt a tug at his sleeve. He turned to see Razor, resplendent in a yellow velvet suit, sitting with a matching pair of leggy blonde girls. Honey hovered nearby. Razor flashed a smile at Mary Ann and nodded to Brew. "I see you been keepin' cool. This your lady?"

Brew stepped around Honey, wondering if it were true that dogs can smell fear. "Yeah. Mary Ann, this is Razor."

Razor stood, bowed deeply and kissed Mary Ann's hand, then stepped back. "Say hello to Sandra and Shana."

"Hi," the girls chorused in unison.

"What are you doing here?" Brew asked Razor.

"What am I doin' here? Man, this is my club. Didn't you know that?" He flashed Brew another big grin. "You play good now."

In a daze, Brew found Mary Ann a seat near the bandstand. As the piano tuner finished, a tall man in glasses and a three-piece suit walked to the microphone and introduced himself as Vice President of Newport Records. He called for quiet, perhaps the first time it had ever been necessary at the Final Bar.

"Ladies and Gentlemen, as you all know, we are recording live here tonight, so we'd appreciate you cooperation. Right now though, let's give a great big welcome to truly one of the giants of jazz, Mr. Bobo Jones and his quartet."

The applause was warm and real as the four musicians took the stand. Bobo, Deacon and Juice were immaculate in matching tuxes. Brew dressed likewise but at the last minute, elected to opt for a white turtleneck sweater. Bobo bowed shyly as the crowd settled down in anticipation.

Brew busied himself with changing the reed on his horn and tried to blot out the image of Bobo leaping from the piano, but there was nowhere to go. He rubbed his throat and tried to smile at Mary Ann as the sound check was completed. It was time.

They opened with one of Bobo's originals, called simply "Changes." Bobo led off with a breath-taking solo introduction that dispelled any doubts about his return being genuine. Then Deacon walked in, bass pulsing quietly while Juice put the cymbals on simmer.

Brew decided that if he survived tonight, he'd just disappear. But now, locked into the music, his fingers flew over the horn in a blur while Deacon's throbbing bass line, pulsing quietly and Juice's drums pushed and prodded and drove him through several choruses. Bobo, eyes closed, head back, nodded and fed Brew the chords with love until at last he backed away and surrendered to the pianist.

Bobo spun out the old magic with a touch so deft he left the audience gasping for breath. This was the second coming of Bobo Jones. Rejuvenated, fresh lines flowed off his fingers effortlessly, transforming the mass of wood and metal and ivory into a complete music entity. Brew listened awestruck and nearly missed his entrance for the final cadenza.

He restated the plaintive theme, then made it his own, twisting and turning the melody before finally returning it safely to Bobo in its original form, and the quartet came together for the final chord.

The applause that rang out and filled the room was deafening. But just as suddenly as it had erupted, it trailed off and lapsed into a tension filled silence. Brew felt it then, his heart pounding, some murmuring as he caught movement near the piano. He turned to see Bobo advancing toward him.

Brew stood frozen, staring hypnotically as Bobo stopped in front of him. As their eyes met in the now hushed room, Bobo wiped away a single tear, then suddenly grabbed Brew and hugged him close.

The audience gradually began to clap again, only one or two people at first, then building into a crescendo as Bobo whispered something in Brew's ear. No one heard what he'd said, and it was later edited off the tape.

Brew wasn't sure he'd heard right at first. Bobo, face cracking into a huge grin, said it again. Brew smiled faintly, then threw his head back, laughing until tears came to his own eyes. Juice was laughing too, and even Deacon smiled. Bobo went back to the piano and the rest of the evening went like a dream.

It was Mary Ann who finally remembered. Everyone was gone except for Manny, who sat in a booth with them. He was already calculating record sales and filling them in on the upcoming tour.

Brew sat slumped down while Mary Ann massaged his shoulders. The Newport people had been all smiles and handshakes and had carted Bobo off to a celebration party. Brew had promised to join them later, but for now, he was content to bask in the luxurious feeling of freedom that washed over him in waves.

"What was it Bobo said to you? After the first number?" Mary Ann asked.

Brew grinned. "'I knew all the time you wasn't Lee Evans, man. Lee was a brother and you sure don't look like a brother.'"

Manny looked up, puzzled, as Brew and Mary Ann both laughed. "I don't get it," he said. "What's so funny about that?"

"Priorities, Manny. It's all a question of your priorities."

"The Resurrection of Bobo Jones," *Bebop, B Flat Scat: An Anthology of Jazz Fiction and Poetry*. Edited by Chris Parker. 1987. Quartet Books.

"The Resurrection of Bobo Jones," *Men From Boys*. Edited by John Harvey. 2003, William Heinemann.

CAMARO BLUE

"Hello?...Yes, I want to report a stolen car...Robert Ware...Oh for Christ's sake...Okay, okay. I don't know when. Last night sometime I guess."

Bobby Ware tried to calm down. He gave his address, the license number and continued to answer questions. "It's a blue, 1989 Chevy Camaro Sport." He listened to the other questions and lit a cigarette.

"It was in front of my house. Oh yeah, there was a horn too...What?...No, not the car horn. A tenor saxophone in a gig bag...What?...Oh, a soft leather case...Yeah that's right...Okay, thanks."

Bobby hung up the phone and sat for a minute, smoking, thinking. "Fuck," he said out loud. "Fuck, fuck, fuck!" He finally gets his dream car and some asshole steals it. Man, I gotta move, he thought. Too much shit in this neighborhood.

He got up, paced around. Barefoot, cut-off jeans, sandals and a Charlie Parker T-shirt, his day time uniform, trying to think who he could borrow a horn from for the gig tonight.

He was working in a quartet at a club on Ventura, backing a singer who was trying to convince everybody that she was the next Billie Holiday but who was not fooling anyone. But hey, a gig was a gig. Three nights a week for three

33

months now, so he couldn't really complain.

He replayed last night in his mind. He'd come home, tired and anxious to get in the house, and had totally spaced leaving his tenor in the car. That wasn't like him or any horn player, but it was too late now. He sat down and turned on the TV, hoping he wasn't going to see his Camaro in one of those car chases the city had become famous for.

When Lisa got home, he was still sitting in front of the TV, watching the news, but there were no stolen car reports and no news from the police.

"Hi, baby," Lisa said. She was carrying a bag from the Lotus Blossom Chinese take-out. "You hungry?" She set the bag down on the kitchen table and walked over to Bobby.

She was in her Century City law office outfit— skirt, blouse, half heels, her hair pulled back in a ponytail. She sat on the arm of Bobby's chair and kissed him lightly on the lips, then let herself slip over the arm on to his lap.

"What's the matter?"

"Somebody stole my car."

"Oh, baby, and you just had it serviced and waxed."

"Tell me about it. But it gets worse."

"What?"

"My horn was in the car."

"Oh no, did you report it?"

Bobby pushed her off him. "Of course I fucking reported it."

Lisa held up her hands. "Okay, okay."

Bobby sighed. "I'm sorry, babe, but you know what the chances are of getting a stolen car back in

L.A.? Especially that car." Bobby had read some-where that Camaros, even older ones, were popular among car thieves. By now, it was probably stripped clean and in a chop shop with somebody was trying to figure out how to put the saxophone together.

For as long as he could remember—at least since high school—Bobby had wanted a Camaro. He could never afford a new one, and good used ones were hard to come by. Then one afternoon, driving back from the store, he'd found this one parked on a side street with a "For Sale" sign in the window. A blue Camaro Sport. One owner, all the service records and looked like it had hardly been driven more than to the store. Now, it was gone.

He took Lisa's Toyota to the gig and had managed to dredge up a tenor from a former student who wasn't sure he wanted to pursue jazz anymore. Bobby had helped him pick out the horn, so it was a good one, but it wasn't Bobby's old Zoot Sims model that he'd bought from a guy on the road in New York.

After the second set, he was standing in the parking lot behind Gino's with the bass player, a tall, thin guy who played well and didn't care anything about singers. They watched a tan Ford Taurus pull in, and two guys in rumpled suits got out and came over.

The bass player cupped the joint in his hand and started walking toward his car. "Cops, man."

"Are you Robert Ware," the older of the two

asked Bobby. The younger one watched the bass player walk away.

"Yeah. Is this about my car?" Bobby wanted to know, but he was wary. They didn't usually send detectives out about stolen cars.

"I'm afraid so," the older cop said, casually showing Bobby his I.D. He looked at Bobby for what seemed like a long time. "We found traces of cocaine in your car, Mr. Ware."

"Oh, not mine," Bobby said. "I'm not into coke."

The younger cop nodded, smiling at Bobby knowingly.

"No, seriously, man. Coke is not my thing." He held up his cigarette. "This is it for me."

The older cop took out a small notebook and flipped through some pages. "Do you know a Raymond Morales? Hispanic male, twenty-nine years old?"

"No."

"You didn't let him borrow your car?"

"Borrow my car...what are you talking about? I don't loan my car to anyone. Ask my girlfriend."

"We did. She told us where to find you."

They all turned and looked as the side door opened and the bass player peeked out. "Hey, man, we're on."

"Listen," Bobby said. "Can you guys wait a bit? We have the last set to do, and then we can talk."

The two cops looked at each other and shrugged. "We'll be at Denny's," the older one said, pointing across the street.

"Cool," Bobby said. "You did find the car, right?"

The younger cop looked at him and smiled again. "Oh yeah."

Bobby found them in a back booth drinking coffee and eating pie. He sat his horn on the floor and slid in next to the younger cop and ordered coffee for himself.

"So? What's the deal on my car? When can I get it back? Was there much damage?"

The two cops glanced at each other. "There was some damage," the younger one said.

"Oh fuck," Bobby said, loud enough that a couple in the next booth turned and looked. "I knew it. Totaled, stripped, what?"

"Bullet holes," the younger cop said.

"What?"

"Mr. Ware," the older cop began. "Your car was involved in a high-speed chase early this morning. Raymond Morales was driving. He apparently ran out of gas. He emerged from your car with a weapon and fired on the pursuing officers. They returned fire, and Mr. Morales was shot at the scene."

"Jesus," Bobby said. He sat stunned, not knowing what to say.

"The driver side door has holes, the window was shattered, and there were several bullets lodged in the seat."

"Is he...?"

Both cops nodded.

"I'm sorry," Bobby said, wondering about Raymond Morales.

"It happens," the younger cop said.

"Your girlfriend said that you reported that there was a saxophone in the car?"

"Yeah, that's right."

"We didn't find it."

Bobby looked at both of them. "What do you mean, you didn't find it?"

"Wasn't in the car," the younger one said.

They talked some more without giving up much information about the incident or when he could get his car back. The older cop gave Bobby his card and said they'd be in touch. They left Bobby to finish his coffee and think about Raymond Morales.

Two days later Bobby got a call from the older cop; Lloyd Foster, Bobby remembered from the business card. "We're done," Foster said. "You can pick up your car tomorrow morning."

"Anything new?" Bobby asked.

"Like what?" When Bobby couldn't think of what to ask, Foster said, "See you in the morning."

Bobby was prepared for the worst when he arrived at the impound garage. Foster and the younger cop were waiting for him. Bobby was surprised to see the car mostly intact. The entire driver side window was gone. The techs had cleaned it out, Foster told him. When he opened the door, he saw the small round holes in the seats where the bullets had lodged.

There were dark spots on the seat—blood stains that hadn't been entirely erased—and there was a strange smell about the interior that Bobby couldn't place. He looked at the two cops.

Foster shrugged. "Techs use all kinds of compounds, liquids to secure evidence, clean. It'll go away eventually."

Bobby nodded and walked around the car. On the passenger door, there were some minor dents and paint scrapings when Morales had side swiped a car, a telephone pole, something in his attempt to get away.

"Why didn't he just, you know, give up instead of trying to shoot it out?"

The two cops exchanged glances and shrugged.

They handed him some papers to sign releasing the car and gave him copies. Then they watched him get in the car and adjust the seat. Morales must have been shorter, as the seat was closer to the wheel than Bobby kept it. He nodded at them and backed the car out of the garage and drove off. In the rear-view mirror, he caught them watching him till he turned the corner.

He pulled into the first available gas station and filled up. He used the Yellow Pages to find a glass repair shop and jotted down the address of two that weren't far away. Ed's Auto Glass was the first.

"We can do it while you wait," the man at the desk said. "What happened? Somebody try to break into your car?"

"Something like that," Bobby said. "It was stolen."

"Wow, and you got it back. Lucky," he said, sliding a clipboard across the counter for Bobby to initial the estimate form. "Give me an hour."

Bobby went for a walk, bought a Coke at a convenience store and smoked, thinking about Raymond Morales dying in his car. He pictured the car, out of gas, skidding to a stop, Morales throwing the door open, him down behind the door, firing at the cops, the glass shattering, bullets embedding in the seat and then Morales falling backwards as a bullet struck him in the chest. He couldn't get the vision out of his mind. All for some cocaine. How much? What was it worth? His life?

He got home ahead of Lisa and went over the car's interior inch by inch, not knowing what he was looking for but unable to let it go. He felt under both seats, up in the springs, in the channel the seat slid back and forth on. He even lay down under it with a flashlight, knowing the cops had already done this but not trusting their thoroughness.

He opened the hatch, raised the flap where the spare tire was kept, took the tire out and felt around the compartment, shined the flashlight everywhere, but it was no go. The car was clean.

The only evidence of the incident was the holes in the seat and the dark stain. Raymond Morales' blood.

"Hey, you got it back," Lisa said, getting out of her car. Bobby hadn't even heard her drive up.

"Yeah." He shut the hatch and locked it as Lisa walked around the car.

"Looks okay," she said.

He nodded and shrugged at her look. "No horn." He opened the driver side door and showed her the bullet holes in the seat, the dark stain.

She just stared. "Jesus, kind of spooky isn't it?"

Bobby got on Lisa's computer and went to the *Los Angeles Time*s web site to check on obituaries. He skimmed through starting with the date after his car was stolen and found it five days after.

Raymond Morales
1974-2004
Beloved son of Angela Morales
Survivors include his sister Gabriela.
A memorial service will be held Wednesday,
May 15 at...

Bobby jotted down the date and time and stared at the photo of Raymond Morales, obviously taken some time a few years before his death. It was almost like a high school yearbook photo. Just a nice looking kid, three years younger than Bobby. He told himself that he was only going out of curiosity, maybe to see if there was a chance someone knew about the horn, but he knew it was more than that.

He drove into Inglewood Park Cemetery and found the site easily. There were at least thirty or more tricked-out low rider cars parked along the curb and a limo. The plain tan sedan that Bobby recognized as Foster's car was also there.

Bobby parked as close as he could and got out. A ways in on the lawn, among the hundreds of tombstones, he saw the small crowd gathered about the gravesite. Foster and the younger cop were standing back from the fringe of the mourners. Foster turned as Bobby walked up.

"Interesting," he said to Bobby. His younger partner turned and smiled.

"What are you guys doing here?" Bobby asked.

"Routine," Foster said. "We know Morales ran with some of these dudes. We're just compiling some information." Foster looked at him. "What about you? Car spooking you?" This made the younger cop smile again.

Several of the young guys turned and glared at Bobby and the two cops. They were all slicked back hair, ponytails, sunglasses, sharply creased chinos and black shirts. A couple started moving toward them but were held back by some others. Bobby moved away to stand by himself.

At the center of the gathering were two women, seated by the casket as the priest finished. Bobby guessed they were the mother and sister. The younger woman raised her eyes briefly and looked at Bobby, then touched her mother's hand.

Bobby turned to look back at the cops as they walked toward their car. He took a deep breath and wondered if this was such a good idea. As the service ended and started to break up, the young guys walked past, stared at him curiously with hate in their eyes and went to their cars. Soon, there was the loud sound of souped-up engines and glass pack mufflers filling the air.

Bobby stood still, hands clasped in front of him, not sure what to do next when Raymond Morales' mother and sister walked by. The sister looked at

Bobby strangely as her mother stopped and looked at Bobby.

"You were a friend of my son's?" she asked, studying his face.

"Well, no, not really," Bobby said, surprised that she spoke to him. "I, ah..."

"High school," Gabriela said. "Taft High School. I know you. Bobby Ware?"

"Yes," Bobby said, taken aback.

Gabriela smiled briefly. "You played a saxophone solo at the school assembly. I was a freshman when you were a senior."

Bobby let his mind travel back ten years. He'd been in the marching band and the jazz ensemble, and he had played at the senior assembly. "Well, yes. I didn't think anybody remembered that."

"Come, Gabby," Raymond's mother said, starting toward the car, already losing interest in Bobby.

Gabriela started after her mother, then stopped and turned. "That was your saxophone, your car, wasn't it?"

Bobby stood mute, realizing she knew everything, watching her dig in her purse for a pen and a slip of paper. She scribbled quickly and pressed it in his hand. "Call me," she said. Then she was gone.

Bobby waited for all of them to clear out. He saw one group of three guys pause at his car and stare, then look over at him before they got in a black Chevrolet and drove off.

* * *

The next morning, Bobby dialed the number. "Barnes and Noble," a voice said. "How can I help you?"

Bobby thought it had been a home number she'd given him but quickly realized she wouldn't have done that.

"Can I speak to Gabriela Morales please?"

"Let me see if she's in," the voice said.

Bobby was suddenly listening to canned music as he was put on hold. It sounded like Dave Koz or David Sanborn, one of those R&B saxes, vamping relentlessly over the same tired chords.

"Hello?"

"Miss Morales? This is Bobby Ware."

"Oh," she said. "I guess you want to talk to me."

"Well, if it's not convenient I can..."

"I have a lunch break at 12:30. There's a coffee place here in the store. We can meet there. This is the big one, on Ventura Boulevard."

"Yeah, okay, that would be fine," Bobby said.

After a pause, she said, "This is strange."

"Yes, it is."

He got there early and took a cup of coffee to the outside tables so that he could smoke. Gabriela appeared a few minutes later.

"Oh, there you are," she said. She was dressed in dark slacks and a white blouse with a plastic B&N nametag pinned to her blouse. Her hair was raven black and framed her face. Very pretty, Bobby thought as he stood up.

She put her hand on his shoulder. "No, don't get up. I'm just going to grab a sandwich," she said. "I'll be right back."

She was back quickly and sat opposite Bobby, a sandwich on a plate and a bottle of water next to it. "Sorry," she said. "I'm on till six. If I don't eat now, well."

"No problem," Bobby said.

She took small bites of the sandwich and studied him. "You don't remember my brother at all, do you?"

"No," Bobby said. "I'm sorry...about what happened."

She nodded and looked down. "He had a lot of problems, and it's not so uncommon. Raymond was lost a long time ago. I remember you," she said, finishing her sandwich. She looked at Bobby's cigarettes on the table. "Can I have one of those?"

"Sure," Bobby said, offering her one. He lit it for her and watched her take a deep drag and cough a little. "Wow, it's been a while. I quit about a year ago."

"Yeah I've quit a couple of times myself."

"I had quite a crush on you," she said, "after I saw you play at the assembly. I used to see you in the halls, by your locker and started going to the games to see you in the marching band."

"Wow, that was a long time ago." Bobby looked away, thinking of the early morning practices, the drilling, the music.

"You still play, right?"

"Yes, I'm working a gig not far from here on weekends."

"That's good. You were talented." She paused. "I remember Raymond wanting to be in the band, but it wasn't cool, you know, that macho shit, so he never pursued it. Maybe, if he had, he would..." Her voice trailed off.

"Look," Bobby said. "I don't want to bother you. I just, I don't know, it's been bothering me. I just had to—"

"See who Raymond was?"

"Yeah, I guess. Since I got the car back, I keep having these visions."

"And there's the horn."

"Well, yes, that too."

She nodded. "I have it in my car. Raymond came home that day, said he'd borrowed the car from a friend. I knew he was lying, but he brought the horn in the house, didn't want anything to happen to it."

"You're kidding."

"No, I think he still thought about playing." She stubbed out her cigarette and glanced at her watch. "I've got to get back to work. C'mon."

He followed her to the parking lot and her car. She opened the trunk. Bobby looked inside and saw the case. He flipped the latches and looked inside. It was like seeing an old friend. He shut the case and took it out of the trunk.

"Thanks, thank you very much."

"Where's your car?"

Bobby hesitated. "Oh, a couple of rows over, but you probably need to go and—"

"I want to see it," she said.

They walked over to his car. Bobby unlocked the door and put his horn in the back.

"Do you mind?" She looked inside.

"No."

Bobby watched her run her hand over the seat, her finger tracing the bullet holes. Bobby shivered. She stepped back, her eyes moist now. "It's kind of closure or something," she said. "Thank you."

"I understand."

She managed a smile. "Well, I guess that's it."

"Would you like to come hear me play?" He blurted it out quickly.

She smiled. "I don't know if that would be such a good idea."

Bobby nodded. "Sure, I understand."

She looked away, then back at him. "But hey, why not? High school crush makes good." She had a beautiful smile, and she gave it all to Bobby.

Bobby gave her the address of Gino's, and they shook hands. She pressed her hand in his. "Thank you," she said, then turned and walked back to the store.

On the way home, Bobby drove by a deserted warehouse with a huge fenced-in parking area. He slowed, then pulled in the open driveway and drove around to the back of the building. He sat for a moment, the car idling, then slammed his foot on the gas pedal. The car shot ahead. He got up to fifty then slammed on the brakes and turned the wheel hard. He threw open the door, stood up, crouched down, stood up again, then threw himself back on the seat, trying to feel the bullet that killed Raymond Morales.

* * *

Eyes closed, leaning back, Bobby circled behind the singer on "Lover Man," looking for his openings, yet not getting in her way. She finished her chorus, and Bobby shuffled toward the microphone and played what he could till the bridge. He stepped aside and saw Gabriela Rosales at a table to his left.

She was leaning forward, her chin resting on her hand, gazing at him with what he guessed was memory. Trying to remember that high school assembly? They finished the set with "Just Friends," and Bobby scorched the small audience with two choruses that got him a phony smile from the singer that said, *Hey, I'm the star, remember?*

He sat his horn on its stand and walked over to Gabriela's table. "So, you made it," he said.

She smiled. "You're much better now than high school."

"Come outside with me," he said. "I need a cigarette."

"Me too." She picked up her purse and put a napkin over her glass.

They walked up Ventura Boulevard a ways, not talking much, just getting used to each other. Finally, they stopped, and she turned to look at him.

"So, where do you think this is going?" she asked. Her eyes were so dark and deep.

He moved in closer and kissed her lightly on the lips. She didn't resist, and when he pulled back, she opened her eyes and looked at him again. "That's what I wanted in high school."

"And now?"

She looked away. "What is this? You want to fuck the kid sister of the guy who was killed in your car?"

"What? No, I—"

She waved her hand in front of her as if she was shooing something away. "I'm sorry. I don't know where that came from. Really, I'm sorry. I don't know why I came really. It's just, I don't know, a connection with Raymond. Does that sound crazy?"

"No," he said. "I think that's why I came to the service. I wanted to see what your brother was about, what his family was about. I don't know if I can keep the car now."

They turned and started walking back toward Gino's. "Raymond was a gangbanger, a cocaine dealer, and he lost. He got in over his head and couldn't get out, except the way he did. I loved my brother, but he gave my mother endless grief and worry. End of story."

"And you?"

"This isn't a good way to start. There must be a girlfriend somewhere, right?"

Bobby nodded. "I live with someone. Two years now."

"Are you in love with her? Are you going to marry her?"

"I don't know," Bobby said. "I thought so."

"I'm not going to be your girlfriend on the side." A glimmer of fire was in her eyes now.

"I know," Bobby said.

She got quiet again, but her hand slipped into his. "We're both here for the same reason," she said.

Bobby knew immediately what she meant. They had both been touched by death, and they were connected by it in a way only the two of them could understand.

"It's maybe the one good thing Raymond did," Gabriela said.

"Yes," Bobby said. "Maybe it is."

"Camaro Blue," *The Cocaine Chronicles*. Edited by Gary Phillips & Jerry Tervalon. 2005. Akashic Books.

FILE UNDER JAZZ

"Man, there it is again," Ray says, reaching for the knob and turning up the volume. "That same damn song."

They're in Lloyd's car, heading down the 405 Freeway toward Santa Monica, mired in lunch-hour traffic. His big, calloused bass player hands on the wheel, Lloyd listens for a minute and shrugs. "It's a minor blues. What's the big deal?"

"The big deal," Ray says, "is I know I've heard it before, but I can't figure out who it is." Ray shrugs. "You know how I am."

Lloyd glances over at Ray. "Yeah, I do. Mr. Obsessive-Compulsive. You won't be happy till you know what the tune is, who's playing, when it was recorded and—"

"Yeah, yeah," Ray says.

"So, call the station," Lloyd says.

Ray listens some more, but it's only the last few bars. The song ends, and they're suddenly blasted by Miles Davis, live at the Blackhawk. He lowers the volume and says, "Maybe I will."

He pats his pocket for his cell phone but remembers he'd left it charging at home. He looks out the window. They'd only moved a few car lengths. The Wilshire Boulevard exit looms mockingly just ahead.

"Think we'll make it?" he says to Lloyd.

"Yeah, we're early," Lloyd says, glancing at his watch.

They're scheduled to hit at one. Some kind of fundraiser scholarship thing, and the organizer is a jazz fan, so it shouldn't be too dumb. The weird part is the location.

"You ever played at a cemetery before?" he asks Lloyd.

Lloyd smiles and lights a cigarette. "No, this is a new one for me."

"Spooky, man," Ray says.

"Hey," Lloyd says, "At least it's not at night."

They find the cemetery and drive in the gates, passing one funeral procession of cars parked along the curb. They drive on, around a long curve to an open area. On a concrete slab, a canopy has been set up and folding chairs arranged in a half circle.

"There we go," Lloyd says, parking his van as close to the tent-like covering as possible. There are a few people milling around already, and Ray sees a large color photograph of a young girl displayed on an easel near the chairs.

They unload Lloyd's bass and Ray's electronic keyboard and amp and begin setting up. A maintenance man appears with a long orange cord and a power strip and shows them where to plug in. Ray gets everything connected, playing a little, testing the sound when the drummer arrives, rolling his drums over to join the setup. Ray doesn't know him, but Lloyd says he plays good. By a quarter to one, they're ready.

It is weird, Ray thinks, looking around at the expanse of green lawn, tombstones and monuments as more people arrive. He takes a short walk, smokes a cigarette, idly looking at the inscriptions on some of the more prominent grave markers. Others are just small plaques in the ground, many overgrown where the grass needs cutting, but one catches his eye.

The grass is neatly trimmed around it, and the plaque is polished. Ray bends down, reads the name. Louis B. Harris, 1935-1967. Somebody misses you, Ray thinks. He straightens up and turns back toward where they'd set up, the strains of that minor blues running through his mind.

More people have arrived now, a fairly respectable crowd. Ray is surprised. He sits at the keyboard and waits for the host to remind everybody why they're here and introduce the trio. Some polite applause follows. Ray nods to Lloyd and, thinking of the little girl, begins with "Sweet and Lovely." He hears Lloyd laugh and say, "Better not play 'Body and Soul' here." Ray hears the drummer chuckle, but the idea sends a chill through Ray.

Later, at home, the tune still haunting him, Ray calls the jazz station. He knows he won't be right until he learns the title and who is playing it. It happens like that every once in a while with Ray. He hears a few bars of something and can't stop till he knows the tune, who recorded it, whatever information he can find.

"KJAZ," the DJ on air answers.

"Yeah," Ray says. "You played something early

this afternoon. I only heard the end, but I was wondering if you remember what it was. Saxophone, some minor blues line."

"I came on at four, man, so you'd have to call back tomorrow and talk to Chuck. He would have been on then. He's on at noon every day."

"Right," Ray says. "Thanks."

He almost counted down the time the next day waiting to call.

"KJAZ."

"Hey, are you Chuck?"

"Yeah, what can I do for you?"

Ray explained.

"Geez, man, I play a lot of things in four hours. I'd have to check the playlist for yesterday."

"Can you do that? It's important."

Ray heard him sigh over the music playing on the studio monitor. "Yeah, I guess. Give me a half hour and call back."

"Thanks," Ray says. He turns on the news but doesn't really focus. He keeps checking his watch then calls again at 2:45.

"KJAZ."

"Hi, I'm the guy that called earlier about the tune you played yesterday."

"Oh yeah. Hang on. I can hardly read my own writing. Okay, it's called 'D Minor Hues.' Done in the sixties sometime I'd guess. Lou Harris, alto player. Don't know what happened to him. Not much info on the LP. Not even the personnel. Just says unidentified piano, bass and drums."

"Did you say Lou Harris?" Ray feels a chill again, thinking of the grave marker. Had to be a different guy. There must have been scores of guys named Lou Harris in L.A.

"Yeah. Hey, I gotta go, man. Going live in a few seconds."

"Thanks," Ray says, but the guy has already hung up.

Lou Harris. Imagine recording an LP and not even getting your name on the record. Ray thinks he's heard the name but isn't sure. He snaps his fingers then, remembers somebody who would know.

Dean Earl was just finishing with a student when Ray looks in. Dean is short with a thick mustache, looking relaxed in a cardigan sweater, slacks and polished loafers. Nearly seventy, he's always reminded Ray of the guy who played George Jefferson on television. Dean spins around on the piano stool. "Hey," Dean says, holding out his hand. "You been being a stranger. Got a lot of gigs, I hope."

"I'm making it," Ray says, slapping Dean's upturned palm. "Got a few minutes?"

"Yeah." Dean glances at his watch. "Nobody till four now. What brings you by?"

"You remember an alto player named Lou Harris? I heard something on the radio yesterday, a minor blues line from an album he did."

Dean's face creases into a frown. "Damn, Lou Harris. Must have been an old one. Lou died long time ago. Yeah I know who he is. Made a few gigs with him."

"Really?" Ray sits down and looks at Dean. "You remember the tune? The DJ says it was called 'D Minor Hues.'"

"Yeah, that's it," Dean says, running his hands through his fuzzy white hair. He hums something, swivels back toward the piano, his fingers searching out the notes.

"Yeah, that's almost it," Ray says.

"Should have been called 'Weird Blues,'" Dean says.

"What do you mean?"

"Bad vibes from that tune. Last thing Lou wrote before he died."

"How did he die?"

Dean looks up at Ray and shakes his head. "Nobody is really sure who did it, but he was shot."

"Jesus," Ray says, feeling a shiver. "Murdered? What happened?"

"Long time ago, man. We were playing this little club in Hollywood, near Shelly's Manne Hole. We finished the set. Yeah, I remember now. That was the last tune we played." Dean shakes his head slowly. "Lou put his horn on the piano, went out the door behind the band stand to have a smoke in the alleyway. I was still talking to the bass player when we heard these two little pops." Dean raises his hand up like a gun, points his index finger. "Pop, pop! We ran out there and found Lou on the ground, blood pouring out of his stomach. We called the cops, but he was gone by the time the ambulance came. They kept us there half the night, questioning everybody."

"They never caught who did it?"

"Nope. Lou had a big eye for the ladies, but he had a wife too. There was one woman always hanging around. I think she was there that night, but in all the confusion, I'm not sure. Everybody thought it was a girlfriend, some woman he'd dropped. Like that gal who shot Lee Morgan at Slugs in New York. Remember that? They'd argued, she went home, came back and shot Lee right there." Dean laughs. "Imagine that, shot at Slugs. Anyway, with Lou, I don't know. Police didn't try very hard. You know how that shit goes, at least then."

Ray nods. Hollywood or South Central Los Angeles. The sixties. The Watts riots still a fresh memory. "Were you on the recording? The DJ said the rhythm section was unidentified."

Dean nods and shakes his head. "They didn't keep very good records then, especially with some little company. No, he'd done that earlier, some little studio, small pressing. Didn't get much airplay or distribution though. Lou was never big."

Dean looks at Ray and frowns. "Why you so interested in Lou Harris? You on one of your missions again?"

"I don't know," Ray says. "I don't know."

But Ray did know. He had to track down that record. He goes online, does the Google thing, checks out Amazon, other sites that list old recordings, reissues, but nothing. Not a mention of Lou Harris anywhere. He calls around to used record stores that he finds in the Yellow Pages, but except for a big place off Hollywood Boulevard, most don't carry much jazz.

"Blue Star," a guy says answering the phone.

"Hey, you carry any real old jazz LPs. I'm looking for a saxophonist named Lou Harris."

The guy just laughs. "Hey, man, I got hundreds. Come in and look for yourself."

With rehearsals and another gig, it's a couple of days before he can make it. Blue Star is in what once must have been an office building. Old posters on the walls, bins of LPs, stacks of CDs on the floor, and all in no apparent order. A monotonous rap band throbs from a sound system somewhere. At the front of the store, sitting at a high desk, is a burly, bearded guy in thick glasses.

"Where's the jazz section?" Ray asks.

The guy points toward the back without looking up from the magazine in front of him. There are three rows of bins with a hand-painted sign on a stick that says "Jazz." Ray sighs and flips through them, scanning titles and names, some Ray has never heard of, some bring back memories. In the "H" section, he finds nothing. The last two bins are labeled "Misc. Jazz."

Ray thumbs through each, stopping occasionally as he recognizes something. Finally, halfway through the second bin, his fingers stop as he stares at the cover. A young black man in a blazer and turtleneck sweater, his arms crossed over an alto saxophone, a cigarette in his mouth, the smoke curling up around his eyes, looks at some point left of the camera. *Lou's Blues* is the title. On the back is a stick-on label in one corner with a penciled price of two dollars and a notation that reads, "File Under Jazz."

Ray slips the record out of the sleeve, handling it carefully. There are some scratch marks, but it's generally in good condition. There's scant information on the back. Another photo of Harris playing, the rhythm section in the background, but is too blurry to recognize anybody. Not even a date—no personnel listing—just the titles of the songs, the record company logo and an address but no liner notes. Track three is "D Minor Hues."

Ray slips the record back in the sleeve, turns to go and almost bumps into a woman standing close by. He hadn't even heard her come up.

She's in her late fifties, early sixties, but still an attractive woman. Slim, dark hair, but her eyes are hidden behind dark glasses. Her clothes are neat but inexpensive. "Are you going to buy that?" she asks, moving over closer to Ray.

"Yeah, why?" Ray asks, the album clutched in his hand almost protectively.

"I used to know him," she says, pointing at the cover photo. "The jazz station played something from it the other day. I thought I'd try to find it. I've been to half a dozen stores."

"Me too," Ray says. "'D Minor Hues.' That one?"

She takes off the glasses, closes her eyes for a moment. "Yes, that's the one." She pauses, opens her eyes, and looks right at Ray. "He wrote it for me." She hums the tune, and Ray feels the hair on the back of his neck stiffen.

They both grimace as the rap recording switches to some heavy metal thing.

"Let's get out of here," Ray says, almost having to shout over the music.

They find a coffee place on Hollywood Boulevard and sit at an outside table. Ray buys them both coffee but takes the album with him when he goes inside. He comes back with the coffee. The woman has taken off the dark glasses and is facing the street, watching the traffic and the people walking by.

Ray sets the coffee down and puts the album on the table. "So, how well did you know Lou Harris," Ray asks, sitting down.

She turns toward him and sips the coffee. "Very well. We were...together for a few months." She glances at the album, puts her hand out. "May I?"

Ray says, "Sure."

She picks it up and stares at the photo of Lou Harris. "Let me buy it from you." She reaches for her purse, a small, scuffed leather bag. "I'll give you twenty-five dollars."

Ray's eyes widen. "I can't do that. I only paid two dollars."

"I know, but it doesn't matter. Are you a collector or something? Is that why you bought it?"

Ray smiles. "No. Piano player. I was just intrigued by the tune. Something about it got to me, and one thing led to another. It happens like that sometimes. It's like, I don't know, an obsession. I called the station, talked to the DJ and my former teacher. He knew Lou as well."

She looks up sharply. "Really? Who?"

"Dean Earl," Ray says.

She nods and smiles. "I'm sorry. I'm Emily, Emily Parker."

"Ray Fuller." He doesn't know whether to shake hands or not, so he sips his coffee and reaches for his cigarettes. "Do you mind?"

"No, not at all."

Ray lights his cigarette, inhales and blows the smoke away from their table.

"Look," she says, "it would mean a lot to me to have this." She taps long slender fingers on the album.

Ray studies her for a long moment. There's something missing, something she's not telling him, but he can't figure it out. "Tell you what," he says, "let me make a tape, and you can have it."

She reaches out and touches his hand. "Thank you. You're very kind."

Ray shrugs. "It's nothing. Really. I was only interested in the tune."

She smiles, more relaxed now. "It is a haunting tune isn't it? That's what Lou called me. Haunting." She colors slightly then and sighs. "Sorry, I don't mean to sound foolish. It was a long time ago."

"How did you meet him?" Ray asks. He watches her, drawn to her in a way he can't explain.

"In a club. I was just bored, driving around and saw the sign that said 'Jazz.' I walked in, heard him play, and sat down, ordered a drink and stayed till closing. He came over once, told me it was brave of me, a white woman coming to a black club. I don't think it's there anymore. I suppose he was right though. The Watts riots hadn't been that long ago."

"And after that?"

"I went every night for the rest of the week. We spent a lot of time together, and then he moved in with me until..." Her voice trails off.

"Until he...died."

"Yes, no, well before that." She closes her eyes again and for a moment is lost in the memory. She blinks then and looks at Ray. "He was murdered, you know."

Ray leans back in his chair. "Yes, Dean told me. Did you know him too?"

She shakes her head. "I must have, but I can't recall his face. Was he playing that night?"

"Yes," Ray says. "It was Dean who found him in the alley. It was never solved?"

"No," Emily says. She puts the dark glasses on again and looks away, watching a teenager roll by on a skateboard.

"Any ideas?"

"Maybe his wife was the cause," she says.

"His wife? Did you tell the police?"

"No, I couldn't. I just...left. I couldn't face it when I heard."

"But why?"

"It didn't matter. Lou was gone, and the police weren't that interested. A black jazz musician, a former heroin user, shot in the alley behind a seedy club. Who would care?"

Ray stubs out his cigarette, drinks off the rest of his coffee and looks at Emily. "You," Ray says.

"It doesn't matter now. It was almost forty years ago."

Ray's mind is swirling with questions. He wants to know everything now, the whole story, but he holds back. "Yeah, I guess."

Emily glances at her watch. "So, how do I contact you, for the album I mean?"

Ray is jolted out of his musing. "Oh, give me a couple of days. I have to find someone with a turntable to record it. I don't have one." He takes out a pen and turns the coffee receipt over to write down her number.

"No," she says. "It's better if I call you."

"Whatever," Ray says, writing his number. "Or," he says, looking at her, "I'm playing Friday night, a solo gig in Santa Monica. Maybe, you could come by? I can give it to you then."

She smiles, hesitates a moment. "Yes, that would be nice. I'd like that."

Ray tells her the name of the club. They both get to their feet. "Okay then. See you Friday. I start at eight."

"I look forward to it. Thank you for the coffee."

Ray watches her walk away till she's lost among other people.

"Spooky, man, really spooky," Ray mumbles to himself.

On Friday night at Bob Burns, Ray is cruising through the first set when Emily Parker walks in.

She takes a seat at one of the stools around the piano bar, orders a drink, and smiles at Ray. The place is pretty full, people jostling for a place, most of the tables full.

He looks at Emily and goes into "D Minor Hues," sees her expression change, her eyes take on a faraway look, then settling on the album resting on top of the piano in front of Ray. He plays it slow, like the record. It's under his fingers now after two days of playing it over and over. He lets the last chord ring for a few moments and looks up. Several people are captivated, and applaud for the first time.

Emily smiles warmly at Ray and nods as he stands up. He slides the album across the piano to her and walks around till he's beside her. "Glad you could make it," he says. "It's all yours." He taps his finger on the album.

"So am I," she says. "That was lovely. It's how Lou might have played it."

He feels a surge of pleasure sweep over him. Now, he knows almost everything. "Be right back," he says. "Gotta make a phone call."

Ray walks to the back and dials the payphone by the restrooms.

"Hello."

"Dean, it's Ray Fuller."

"What's up, Ray? You caught me nodding off in front of the TV."

"The girlfriend of Lou Harris. Was her name Emily Parker?" Ray waits impatiently for Dean's answer, looking back toward the piano bar, but he can't see Emily.

"Man," Dean says, "so long ago, but, yeah, I think that's right. How did you—"

"Thanks, Dean. I gotta go." Ray hangs up and walks quickly back to the bar, but Emily Parker is gone and so is the record. In its place is a folded piece of paper propped on the keyboard, a note in neat, careful handwriting. Ray goes outside, looks up and down the street, but there's no sign of Emily Parker. He thinks of checking the small parking lot but he doesn't know if she came by car.

He lights a cigarette and reads the note:

Ray,

I guess you've figured it out by now. Lou was going back to his wife, and I couldn't allow that. It was the only way. Don't try to find me. I'll remember you though for your kindness.

Emily

Ray stands numbly, reading the note over several times. Of course, it was her. Lou Harris wouldn't have gone outside by himself with Emily there. She must have gone out the front, circled around to the alley, come up to Lou, pleaded her case maybe one last time before she slipped the gun out of her purse, pushed it against Lou's chest, like she was going to kiss him, and shot him instead. The two little pops Dean said he'd heard. She would have been gone before anybody came out. Was that how it went down?

Ray feels sick suddenly. His hand shakes,

holding the note, realizing what he's done. He slips the note in his pocket and goes back inside and sits down at the piano. What should he do? Take the note to the police? How would he make anybody understand?

"Hey, piano man?" A husky guy at the bar with a blonde on his arm looks at Ray. "What was the name of that last tune you played?"

Ray looks up. "What?"

"That song you played, just before the break. What's the name of it?"

"'D Minor Hues,'" Ray says, knowing he'll never play it again.

"File Under Jazz," *A Merry Band of Murderers*. Edited by Claudia Bishop & Don Bruns. 2006. Poisoned Pen Press.

GRACE NOTES

Noel Coffey stared out the window of his Hamburg hotel room, listening to the November rain—falling relentlessly since late afternoon—beat erratic rhythms against the glass. Noel watched it wash the streets, blur the neon glow from the restaurant sign across the narrow road and slash against the window. He tried to put time to the rhythm. Definitely up, some bebop standard, patterns that would give even Thelonious Monk fits. It made Noel think of an opener for that night. Something up, buoyant, something that would floor everyone.

He sighed and turned away from the dark, wet night outside, reluctant to leave the warmth and safety of his room. The German sparseness appealed to him: clean, simple, functional, nothing more than needed and only a short walk to the club.

He dug for cigarettes in his shirt pocket. He lit one and glanced at his horn lying on the bed. The Selmer Mark VI tenor saxophone gleamed in the harsh glare of the light that burned from a square over the bed like a baby spotlight. Waiting, expectant but fearful, like some unrequited lover who wonders if the affair might be over.

Noel stared at the horn. He had only to fill it with his breath, touch its keys to bring it to life. He sat down on the bed and cradled the horn, listening in his mind to the music it could play, the music he could play like he had this afternoon. He sat quietly, smoking for a few moments, then took the horn apart and stuffed it into its soft leather case, his hands shaking only slightly as he zipped up the case. He grabbed the half empty bottle of Schnapps off the nightstand and took a long pull. It burned his throat and settled like fire in his stomach.

Shit. It had all gone out the window during the rehearsal earlier this afternoon.

The rhythm section hadn't been near as bad as he'd feared. Earlier that afternoon, after the briefest of introductions, Noel had run them through some standards, a couple of blues lines, not pushing, just being comfortable, blowing easy, laying back, saving it for tonight.

Can't scare these German dudes, Noel thought, remembering Aaron's parting words.

They know you, man. Noel Coffey is a name, a bad tenor player. They got your records; they remember how it was with the quartet, so jus' be cool, man. You got nothin' to prove.

But Noel had a lot to prove, and despite Aaron's encouragement, he hadn't been sure. He'd nodded, hugged Aaron and boarded the night train from Paris, a slow journey that left him far too much time to think.

No, the rhythm section hadn't been bad. The drummer, a stout man with probing eyes, had bugged him all during the rehearsal, staring at Noel like he was some kind of freak. What are you looking at? Noel wanted to scream at him. Haven't you ever seen an ex-junkie? The bassist had just sat on a bar stool, his arm cradled around his instrument, watching Noel warily. Only the pianist was cool, a studious-looking cat with thick glasses, a touch like Bill Evans.

"Your work with Miles was very fine," the pianist had said almost reverently when they'd spoken briefly on a break.

Yeah, so fine he'd only lasted six months. One record though, Noel reminded himself, trying desperately to dredge up confidence. There was no denying that, the vinyl proof of his ability to hold his own with a legend. The other recordings with The Quartet spoke for themselves.

The Quartet. There was The Modern Jazz Quartet, and The Dave Brubeck Quartet, but Noel, Calvin, Billy and Ellis had simply been The Quartet. Four young lions storming onto the jazz scene with youthful exuberance, phenomenal talent and a healthy respect for the past. They'd headlined clubs and festivals, recorded four albums, and then, as is so often the case, their success was over as quickly as it had begun. Each of them had gone his separate way. Where were they all now, Noel wondered.

After two years of scuffling in Europe, Noel had lost track of the others except for bits and pieces of news he got from two-month-old copies of *DownBeat* or when some of the New York guys came over on tour.

Ellis, who had tired of the road, was apparently getting a foothold in Hollywood: writing jingles, scoring for movies and TV. Calvin was gigging around the city, or on the road for whoever paid the tab. Billy was becoming a rock star, the most swinging drummer this side of Art Blakey, playing in a fusion band behind a no-talent, gravely-voiced singer in jeans, a head band and a tie-died T-shirt. Noel shook his head and smiled at the thought. Billy would dig the groupies.

Noel shook off the past, went into the bathroom and splashed cold water on his face. He leaned on the sink, staring at his reflection in the mirror as if there were some answer in the once youthful face. He dried off, shrugged into a wrinkled trench coat and grabbed his horn. Time to go.

He pulled the door closed behind him and walked downstairs to the street. Outside, he glanced up at the dark sky, felt the rain on his face, then ducked around the corner to the club. He paused at the entrance to the Jazzhaus, taking in the paper banner taped to the window with the hastily scrawled lettering.

"LIVE RECORDING—TONIGHT ONLY— NOEL COFFEY"

They might be right, Noel thought as he pushed through the door and made his way to the small bandstand.

He unpacked his horn and laid it carefully on the top of the piano, nodded to the bassist and drummer, who stopped talking when he approached. He got off the stage quickly. They look worried, Noel thought. Did they think I wasn't going to show up?

He took a seat by himself at the end of the bar and ordered a double Schnapps. He lit another cigarette and looked around the room. It was filling up quickly with people who brought in with them the smell of wet coats and hair as they shook off umbrellas, talked loudly and glanced toward the bandstand.

The jazz freaks were already taking up the front tables. Pseudo hipsters, nodding their heads, snapping their fingers off the beat to the taped music, their eyes hidden behind dark glasses. We're hip, their poses said. Noel could feel their glances, their eyes on him, the whispered comments and the air of anticipation.

Noel had never played Germany. Paris, Ronnie Scott's in London, all over Scandinavia. He'd been well-received, and there was no doubt the fans were knowledgeable, appreciative. Why else would so many American jazz musicians be here? Noel was simply following in the footsteps of Sidney Bechet, Dexter Gordon, Chet Baker and the scores of musicians who had found that Europeans dig jazz. Shit, Johnny Griffin and Art Farmer were still living here. But Noel had never been to Germany, so tonight, the fans were out in force to hear, "One of the better young tenor players in jazz." At least that's how the press release read.

There was no doubt about it, Noel thought. Playing jazz was a strange occupation, and playing it well cost a lot. Noel had paid his dues, and now, he was heavily in debt. Jazz had ravaged his body, damaged his soul and made him an outcast, an exile from his own country, maybe, even from himself.

Until today, he'd been straight for nearly two months. No junk, no booze, just practicing every day, eating right, taking long walks, even sitting in a couple of times at one of the Paris after-hours spots; trying always, desperately, to recall how he used to sound. That was the hard part. Getting it back slowly. Now, he was ready. Maybe.

The technicians from the radio station crept around the stage, busily running cables, setting up the remote recording gear. One of them tapped a microphone and walked over to where Noel sat. He smiled at Noel, "It will be good, yes?"

Good for what, Noel wondered. Jesus, he wasn't ready. He shouldn't have listened to Aaron. It was humid in the club, and the warmth of the Schnapps burned his throat as he downed another glass. He felt the pain in his gut start again. It wouldn't go away. It was more than withdrawal. It was...fear. What if he couldn't play? It always came back to that same question.

He jerked his mind off the thought, let his eyes roam around the club, then settle on a young blonde woman at one of the front tables. She was sitting with another older woman. Bet you'd like to blow Coffey's horn, huh? He caught her eye and flashed the practiced smile he knew always had the same effect. She smiled back self-consciously, then quickly averted her eyes, turned away, obviously uncomfortable at being singled out.

Noel felt a hand on his shoulder. "You are ready, yes?" It was Freddie, a former trombonist and the owner of the Jazzhaus. When Noel didn't answer, Freddie's eyes went to the glass in Noel's hand.

"Don't worry, Fritz, you'll get your money's worth," Noel said, unable to keep the hostility out of his voice. Freddie shrugged.

"Good. I will announce now." He left Noel at the bar and conferred briefly with the recording technicians, then stepped toward the microphone. Somebody turned off the taped music, and Noel could feel the audience settle down as he ambled toward the stage, brushing by the blonde. He smiled at her again, mounted the stage and walked over to the pianist, who was waiting expectantly.

Noel thought for a moment and decided to play it safe. "'Blues in F'," he whispered. Yes, a medium tempo blues to loosen up, take it easy. He began to snap his fingers for the tempo over Freddie's introduction.

The applause was brief. The room quieted and suddenly, the only sound was Noel's snapping fingers. Well, fuck it. Let's get it over with. He counted them in, and while the rhythm section played a couple of choruses in front, he clipped the horn on the chain around his neck. He looked down and winked at the blonde and stepped up to the microphone.

Feet planted firmly, he closed his eyes and imagined the hundreds of times he'd been on stage with The Quartet, blocking out everything else from his mind. He put the horn to his lips, tasted the reed, listened to the pianist laying down the changes, the pulse of the bass, the high-pitched cymbal of the drummer. It wasn't Billy Dean or

Calvin, or Ellis, but they were there, laying down a smooth rhythmic carpet for Noel to walk on.

He took a breath and then his mind suddenly drifted into confusion. He couldn't focus. What were they playing? A blues? Easy now. Listen. He pressed a key on the horn, gathered some breath and blew, but no sound came out. Nothing. He frowned, tried again, but the horn just squeaked in protest. Humidity, that was it. He twisted the mouthpiece. The reed was too damp. He squeezed his eyes shut, tried again, felt droplets of sweat breaking out on his forehead.

This time, only a squawk, then nothing but air escaping his lips. The sound evaporated in the air. He opened his eyes in panic. Not this too. Not this too. Come on. Come on. Think.

He stared at the blonde in front. A pained expression crossed her face. She glanced at her friend, put her hand to her mouth. She knows, Noel thought. He scanned the other faces in front of him. They all know. What was wrong with the goddamn horn? He wheeled around, turning his back on the audience. The rhythm section, glancing at each other, started another chorus and then stared back at Noel, puzzled and afraid. He felt a wave of nausea sweep over him.

He spun around, facing the audience again. What were they all looking at? He stepped toward the microphone once more, stumbled and nearly fell, then righted himself by grabbing the stand with one hand.

He called over his shoulder to the pianist. "Keep playing, man. Keep playing."

Through the haze of smoke, he caught another glimpse of the blonde, leaning forward, frowning at him. Whatta you expect, bitch? Isn't this what you came for? I can't do it. That's right, baby. You're seeing it live. Noel Coffey, fucking up badly, totally unable to play a simple blues in F or even get a sound out of his fucking horn. Oh, God, why did I let Aaron talk me into this?

He gripped the horn tightly with both hands, choking it, suddenly wanting to smash it on stage. Man, it was time to go home, to New York or L.A. He made another grab for the microphone as another wave of nausea and dizziness swept over him. Jesus, he was going to throw up. He choked back the bile and stared at the crowd, dropped his hands to his sides in surrender. The horn hung around his neck like a useless appendage. He grabbed for the microphone again with both hands.

He felt himself begin to tremble. A hand touched his shoulder. He wheeled around and found the face of the pianist. When had they stopped playing? He jerked away. The shaking got worse. The he looked down helplessly as a warm dark stain began to spread over the front of his trousers.

Noel began to cry soundlessly, feeling the tears stream down his face.

He blinked them away and focused on the blonde again. She was half rising out of her chair, one arm outstretched, her face contorted in pain. Noel kept his eyes on her even as he pitched forward off the bandstand and crashed into her table.

He fell on his horn. His mind registered breaking glass, cries, chairs scraping and all he could think was, Charlie Parker, you motherfucker, this is all your fault.

"Grace Notes," *Blue Lightning*. Edited by John Harvey. 1998. Slow Dancer Press.

JAZZLINE

"This is WJAM, your jazz spot for the Valley, 105.1 on your FM dial. I'm Tim Weston, and it's time for 'Round Midnight'."

Weston eased up the volume on the Duke Ellington record spinning on turntable one, waited a few seconds, then faded the music and continued his lead-in announcements. "I'll be with you till three this morning with some of the best in modern jazz, so relax, get comfortable and in the groove. If there's anything special you'd like to hear, remember, we do take requests. Just give Jazzline a call at 555-2929, and I'll do my best to find it for you, right here on WJAM."

Weston returned the gain to normal levels and clicked off the air microphone. He removed the headphones and began searching through a stack of new CDs for the latest release from Stan Getz, glancing at the phone light as he did.

Was she going to call again, he wondered.

There were four lines into the studio, but no more than one at a time ever lit up on Weston's shift. None of the lights glowed at the moment.

He cued up two CDs and filled in the needle drop sheet, the listing of artist and the cut he would play next. First break was at 12:20, so he had time to pull the Public Service Announcements and ready the commercial cartridges.

He stretched, leaned back in the swivel chair, laced his hands behind his neck and listened to Stan Getz glide through the changes of "Stella by Starlight." He faced the control board of slide dials, microphone buttons, and a large clock. To his left were two turntables; to the right, stacked on top of each other, two compact disc players and the tape cartridge machines.

He always felt curiously cut off from the outside world on these late shifts, like the pilot of a space capsule. The only link to the outside was the phone. He tried to imagine callers, the listeners of his show. After six months, he had a substantial following of night owls, insomniacs, musicians and jazz buffs. He pictured them crashed on couches, lying in bed, pacing off early morning hours in solitude or driving around town.

When they called, he made a game of putting faces to the voices. There were a lot of regulars, and some, like Weston, were knowledgeable jazz fans. The lonely ones just wanted to talk. Weston could always tell which ones knew the music.

But *her* voice. She was the one he thought about most, the easiest to imagine, to put a face and a body to, even if he still didn't know her name. Weston caught the phone light winking at him.

"Jazzline."

"Hi, lover, you're cooking tonight." She'd called several times in the past few weeks, then the calls mysteriously stopped. Weston had gone crazy wondering if she'd call again, wondering what she looked like, and if he'd ever meet her.

"Where have you been?" he asked. He eyed the

timer on the CD player. Still a minute and forty-seven seconds left before the next break.

"I've been working up the nerve to call you again and tell you...what I really want." Her voice had a smoky, throaty sound that reminded Weston of Julie London.

He gripped the phone tighter and smiled. "Tell me."

"I want us to meet. At my place," she said, her voice quieter than usual. "Tonight."

"Hey, baby, I'd like nothing better, but you know I'm here till three."

"I know that. I mean after. After you get off, you could come over here."

"Where is here?" Only thirty-eight seconds until the break. "Can you hold while I do some business?"

"Well, I guess."

Weston stabbed the hold button on the phone, put it down, slipped on the headphones and pulled the microphone into position as the CD finished.

"Stan Getz and the Quartet on WJAM, your jazz station for the Valley," he said. "We'll be back with some more music in a moment but first, these important messages." He pressed the button for the tape cartridge, a thirty-three second safe-sex message, and grabbed the phone.

"Hey, I don't even know your name."

She was gone. He listened to the dial tone, then slammed down the phone as the spot finished. He read two more PSAs, then played one of the records he had cued up for the next segment of the show.

He clicked on the mic, then read off the album cover of his next selection.

"All right you piano lovers, next up we've got some Oscar Peterson and his Trio, live at the London House in Chicago." With the word Chicago, he pressed the remote button for the turntable, and Peterson's piano simultaneously filled the headphones and the airways. He turned down the mic volume, flipped the cutoff switch and glanced at the clock facing him. This track ran almost nine minutes. Why couldn't she call now?

Seconds later, the phone light blinked again. He grabbed for it. "Jazzline."

"Weston, why don't you quit playing that nigger music?" Weston recognized this voice too, a regular. At first, just annoying and now, impossible, a caller who had bugged him for weeks. Not enough big bands, then it wasn't enough standard tunes or enough ballads and now this.

"Stan Getz is a white artist," Weston tried. "I just played him. Jazz is black music, you know."

"Don't lecture me, Weston. I've forgotten more about jazz than you'll ever know." The man began coughing so hard he was unable to continue.

"Why don't you know enough to give up those cigarettes and while you're at it, my show." He slammed down the phone.

Station policy or not, this guy was a creep, and Weston didn't mean to listen to him anymore. He cued up the next record, a track from the Woody Herman band and waited. Two minutes into "Four Brothers," the phone lit up again.

"Jazzline."

"I'm sorry I hung up, but I couldn't talk. My husband came in, but he's gone now."

"Husband?" I knew there had to be something wrong, Weston thought.

"Yeah, he's usually not up at this time. I listen to you alone, with earphones. It's like your voice is in my head."

Weston considered. Sexy voice, interested, but married. Problems, complications. Probably wasn't going anywhere. "So, you were going to tell me your name, where you lived."

"Madeline," she said quickly. "I can't talk now, he's coming back." Before Weston could protest, she hung up again.

He looked at the phone, shook his head and replaced it in the cradle. A kook? He put on two more long tracks and busied himself with the other late-night work: cataloging some of the discs, logging in level readings and the FCC report for operator on duty.

By two o'clock he was caught up and had all the music lined up for the rest of the show.

"Tim Weston with you for one more hour on WJAM. We're going to keep it slow and dreamy this last hour with some solo piano, some Miles and a ballad from Carmen McRae. First though, this message." He pushed the cartridge button for another PSA and cued up Keith Jarrett.

"All right, here we go until three." Miles Davis' mournful trumpet filled his headphones. He eased down the microphone and clicked off just as the phone light glowed again.

"Jazzline."

"Sorry I couldn't talk before. He came back, forgot something." She sounded out of breath.

"It's okay." He paused. "Are we really going to meet or—"

"Yes. Yes. You don't know how much the music you play means to me. It's like...I don't know, like..." Her voice trailed off huskily. Weston could fill in the blanks, imagine her lying on a plush couch in a negligee, eyes closed, sipping white wine.

"He's...we're not really married. We just live together, but I don't—"

Weston eyed the CD timer. A minute fourteen seconds to go before another break. "Look, if you want, I could come by in the afternoon, or maybe we could meet somewhere else."

"No, it has to be tonight." Weston heard the desperation in her voice.

"Okay, but where?" He listened and copied down the address and watched the seconds tick away. She hung up almost simultaneously with the record's end. He cued up the next track and noticed the phone light blinking again. Had she forgotten something, changed her mind?

"Jazzline."

"Jesus, Weston, don't you have any big bands down there? No Benny Goodman. No Woody Herman. Or how about some Stan Kenton?"

Weston sighed. "Look, I don't know what you want," he said, "but if you're so unhappy, why don't you change the station or watch TV?"

"'Cause I like bugging you, Weston." He stopped then, seized by another coughing spasm and hung up.

At 2:50, Weston made his final break and buzzed in the relief DJ. What a night.

The Cove Apartments was a huge complex. It took him several minutes of long walks, wrong turns and dead ends before he finally found 1151. He'd almost given up. Was this just a little bit crazy or what? Was he really going to do this? He had to be crazy. Well, I might as well see what she looks like, he thought.

There was just one light on that he could see as he rang the bell. The door opened just a crack. It was dark inside. "Tim? Come in."

It was her all right. There was no mistaking that voice. Weston stepped inside and closed the door behind him. Then he heard someone cough.

"Yeah, come in, Weston," the other voice said. He recognized that one too.

"Jazzline," *Ellery Queen Mystery Magazine.* March 1991. Davis Publications, Inc.

MATINEE

"Idiots. I'm dealing with idiots," said Arthur Webb. He turned to look out from his tiny cubicle office on the third floor of the humanities building. Scattered across his desk was the latest response in his attempt to market his detective novel.

The manuscript was in tatters. Several pages were missing and others were marred with coffee stains and cigarette burns. Stapled to the title page was a form rejection with one word hastily scribbled beneath the signature: "Derivative!!!" The editor had seen fit to underline the word several times, as if the exclamation marks were not enough.

Derivative? Webb was outraged. Were all the editors in New York cretins? Angrily, Webb glanced at the other results of his efforts stacked on the floor near his desk. In his wildest dreams, Webb had never imagined the difficulty he would encounter in finding a publisher or agent, much less selling it.

He leaned back in his chair, running his hands through his steel gray hair. The idea had come to him full-blown on a day when he was besieged by term papers and requests by students to discuss their grades before upcoming exams. Webb had been so sure it couldn't miss. How? How could they not see?

In preparation, he had read, studied and literally

dissected hundreds of detective novels for style, plot and character development until he felt sure the genre was second nature. After all, for a professor of Eighteenth Century literature, who analyzed and taught complex works for a living and who had been published in the *MLA Journal* several times, this was child's play. Most of the books he'd read *he* had found derivative and sadly lacking in any literary merit. Tough guys, wise-cracking private eyes, feminist radicals, bungling amateurs and cozy suburban murder mysteries that were no more than updated versions of Agatha Christie. It was they who were derivative. Webb's would be not only original but also well written.

How could a novel about a transgender detective who solves a murder be derivative? Webb reviewed the plot in his mind once again. A man's wife is murdered. He undergoes a sex change operation, dates the suspected killer he uncovers after an exhaustive and clever investigation and finally gets him—or her, Webb wasn't sure which—to admit to killing his wife. It was brilliant, topical and executed with elegance, at least in Arthur Webb's mind.

Once underway, Webb had written with a fury, an all-consuming passion that left his colleagues and students to wonder about his sanity, and his wife, Janet, totally confused and frightened. Every hour he could spare from his schedule was spent in pursuit of the novel's completion. He found himself waking in the middle of the night to scribble some note about the plot, an incident of one of the characters or merely some piece of description.

By end of the term, exams and papers graded, the novel was ready. Webb carefully typed in the final draft on his new computer and made several photocopies—courtesy of the English department's machine—and then one day in June, he sat down to map out his marketing strategy. He bought a market directory of publishers and agents and studiously noted submission requirements. He clipped articles from writer's magazines, haunted the bookstores, noting which publishers bought detective novels and finally narrowed down the field to ten.

Next, he assembled his materials: a dazzling array of padded envelopes, labels, cardboard backing sheets and packaged five sets of the manuscript for submission. He wrote cover letters and marched triumphantly to the post office.

Later the same night, he took his wife to his favorite restaurant where they had a splendid dinner of seafood pasta accompanied by a superb Sonoma County Merlot. He sipped the wine and settled back, mused in anticipation, secure in the knowledge that a contract and sizable advance would soon find its way to his mailbox. Perhaps even a phone call from an editor, singing the praises of his book and inviting him to New York at his convenience, all at their expense, of course. But now, alone in the sparse confines of his office, Arthur Webb's fantasies were shattered.

Two of the five had come back unopened with a brief note stating that these publishers did not accept unsolicited submissions. Wrong. Webb double-checked his directory and put it down to changes in editorial policy. The post office lost one copy and all that was returned was his address label. How could two hundred and seventy-two pages of perfectly typed manuscript, each page with his name, just disappear?

Number four arrived in tatters—not even in the return mailer Webb had provided—but instead, in a cheap manila envelope. The last was returned intact with a puzzling note: "Enjoyed this very much. We wish the publisher who buys it all the luck."

Why didn't they buy it then? What was wrong with these people?

And now this. Derivative! The word stared back at Webb, mocking him. Slamming his fist down on his desk, Webb stood and paced around his office. No longer trusting the U.S. mail, careless editors and the charlatans of the publishing world, Webb decided he would make five more copies of his masterpiece and buy a round-trip ticket to New York. He, Arthur Webb, would storm the big apple himself. He forgot, at least for the moment, that he was scheduled to go to New York anyway. He frowned. There was that business with Pearson.

For a moment, he let his mind slip to the other reality of his life. Making assignments to Pearson was never pleasant. The man had this annoying air of superiority about him, although his reputation was obviously well deserved. Pearson had never failed.

He shook off these thoughts, gathered his things together and went home to announce his decision

to Janet. She thought he was having a breakdown.
"You're going where?" she said.

Webb was already in the departure lounge when
he remembered. Well, remembered wasn't exactly
right. What he knew was he'd forgotten something.
What that something was, he realized with a twinge
of panic, he had no idea.

He glanced around at the other waiting
passengers as if they could somehow remind him of
what it was he'd forgotten. His big suitcase was
checked, and the small carry-on bag sat on the floor
in front of him. He patted the inside pocket of his
blazer for his ticket and boarding pass, felt for his
wallet. No, it was something else.

He listened to the public address system
announcements and checked his watch. There was
time to call, but who would he call? Janet wouldn't
be home yet, which was precisely why he'd booked
this flight. He'd be on his way, touching down at
JFK before she got home to see that he was gone
and find the note. He could hear her voice in his
head now.

"You just fly off to New York and leave me a
note?" Janet would shout to the empty house.

He watched one of the attendants on the desk
pick up a microphone and make the boarding
announcement. Well, at least the flight was going to
be on time. At least Janet hadn't come home early.
At least she hadn't had him paged to argue the
point once again. He looked around quickly, feeling
suddenly like someone on the run, like Pearson

perhaps. No, Pearson was too calm and cool to ever feel like that. God, what a way that would be to live, he thought as he made his way to the gate and surrendered his boarding pass to the smiling attendant.

As soon as they were airborne, Webb ordered a drink. He poured Scotch out of a miniature bottle, let it trickle over the ice in the plastic glass and ate a couple of peanuts, although as usual he had trouble getting the damn bag open.

Next to him, a man in a dark suit and tie was going through the contents of his briefcase, a slim aluminum thing that looked to Webb like it might be used for transporting ransom money. Webb watched him, fascinated. The man smiled briefly at Webb and eventually fished out a small handheld calculator. "Thought I'd forgotten it," he said.

Webb nodded but ignored the man. He didn't want to talk to anyone. What was it? What had he forgotten? Whatever it was, there was no going back now. It nagged him, but with everything he'd planned in the last few days, he might be forgiven a slip or two, although that was not at all in character for Arthur Webb.

After what seemed like only minutes, he could feel the plane descending into New York and heard the usual announcements about seat belts, tray tables and personal belongings.

Webb was one of the first off, as if there might be some penalty for staying on board longer. He pushed through the crush of people and looked for the sign to baggage claim. Then he heard the public address system.

"Arthur Webb, please pick up the white courtesy phone. Arthur Webb."

Webb stopped in his tracks at the sound of his name and began looking for a phone. He found a bank of courtesy phones further down the corridor and picked one up. "Arthur Webb."

"Arthur?"

"Janet?"

"That wasn't very nice, dear, just taking off like that."

Webb slapped his hand on the wall above the phone and looked at the poster of a woman who stared down at him. "Oh my God," he muttered to himself, suddenly remembering what he'd forgotten as he stared at the woman's face on the poster. It was an advertisement for a Broadway show.

"Arthur? Are you there?"

"Janet, listen to me. On the hall table, is there an envelope that—"

"Yes, that's why I'm calling. I thought you might need it. There's no address on it, but it's sealed with tape. Shall I open it and read—"

"NO!" Webb shouted. He shuddered at the thought of Janet opening the envelope. Two other callers looked at him with raised eyebrows. "Listen to me, Janet. Don't touch it. Don't open it. Take it to FedEx and send it overnight to me immediately. Do you understand?"

"No need to shout, Arthur"

Webb rubbed his forehead. "Just do it, Janet. Right now, before you do anything else." He quickly gave her the name of the hotel he had reserved.

"All right, Arthur. Calm down. I will."

"Remember, don't open it. I'll call you later."

Webb hung up the phone, wiped the perspiration beading his forehead and headed for baggage claim.

At the same moment that Arthur Webb walked toward baggage claim, Pearson strolled through the West Village, enjoying the good weather, letting his whims take him where they would, catching the eye of a woman now and then, and glancing in shop windows.

He stopped in front of a used bookstore, and a book of jazz photographs caught his eye. He took off his sunglasses and stepped inside. A bell tinkled overhead, announcing his arrival. He nodded to the clerk, who looked up as he headed for the window display. Lifting the book from an acrylic stand, he gingerly thumbed through the pages of an old collection by William Claxton, who had begun his career photographing Gerry Mulligan and Chet Baker. The book was in excellent condition. Pearson smiled and knew he had his find for the day. He opened the book to the first page and noted the penciled price and smiled again.

He started for the front desk, then paused. "Is there a cookbook section?" he asked.

The clerk nodded. "In the back, on the left. It's marked."

"Thanks," Pearson said. He made his way to the back of the store and found two bottom shelves of cookbooks. He knelt down and quickly scanned the titles. His pulse quickened. Sometimes it happened like this. He ran his finger across the books and then stopped. There. A collection of recipes compiled by famous and not-so-famous jazz musicians. Scanning over the table of contents, his eye came to rest on a salmon recipe by vocalist Annie Ross.

"Yes," Pearson whispered to himself. He closed the book and headed back to the front where the clerk was just finishing a transaction with another customer. Pearson waited patiently and then stepped forward. "I'll take these two," he said.

The clerk noted the price of each book and glanced up at Pearson. "Charge?"

"Cash," Pearson said.

"No haggling?" The clerk allowed himself a small smile.

"I never bargain for something I want," Pearson said, not smiling at all.

In minutes he was back out of the bustling streets of the Village. He decided to go back to his hotel and wait for Webb's call and decide whether tonight would be the Blue Note, Bradley's, or the Village Vanguard.

It was going to be an all jazz day.

Pearson studied the photo and looked up at Webb. "She's very pretty," he said. "Kind of a shame."

Webb gave him a bemused look. "That's not like you to be concerned." He shook his head. "Anyway, you'll be long gone. The rest of the information—schedules, hangouts, friends—is in the envelope. There's even a copy of the script, if you thank that will help."

Webb had spent the afternoon haunting the front desk of his hotel, pacing, checking every half hour for FedEx deliveries, sure Janet would have botched the sending of the envelope. He still couldn't believe he'd forgotten to bring it with him. How would he have explained that to Pearson? Pearson had flown in from who knows where, and he was so expensive. To make the trip for nothing would have cost everyone. Webb shuddered at the thought. But it had arrived. He must pick up something for Janet, perhaps have her join him, take in a show. He suddenly became aware of Person looking at him.

"Sorry, what did you say?" He watched Pearson study the photo again, probably memorizing her features—cascading blonde hair, greenish eyes and skin too smooth for a woman over forty, if the rest of Webb's information was correct, and Webb knew it was.

"Deadline. I said deadline." Pearson repeated.

"Oh, of course." Webb cleared his throat. "We'd like it, ah..." Webb searched for the word. "Attended to by Wednesday. There's a matinee at two. Maybe before or after that?" His eyebrows rose questioningly.

Pearson nodded and slipped the photo back in the envelope. They were in the Blue Note, one of Pearson's favorites. He took another bite of his salmon, leaning back, savoring the flavor of the mesquite grill, the seasonings, aware of Webb watching him, waiting for his answer. He took a sip of the chilled Chardonnay and nodded at Webb.

"Shouldn't be a problem. I have some business in Boston, but I have to be back on Thursday anyway, so I'd like to wrap this up as soon as possible."

Webb's sigh was audible. "Splendid," he said. "I'll pass along the word." He downed the last of his wine and put his hands on the table as if to go.

He hated that despite the fact that he had dispatched Pearson a number of times, he never knew what the man was thinking. In fact, he knew nothing about him—not even his first name—except for a phone number, and he guessed that was an untraceable cell phone. It was always a different number.

Pearson put his hand on Webb's arm. "Not yet. I want you to hear this group." He glanced toward the bandstand where a bassist was leaning over the piano, striking a key, plucking a string on his bass, tuning up, joking with the drummer, who was attaching cymbals to the stands. "There's a new young tenor player and a pianist," Pearson said.

Webb leaned back. He had hoped to escape before the music started. Jazz was not his pleasure, and Pearson always made such a big deal about it. America's classical music, he called it.

"You know why I like jazz so much?" Pearson didn't wait for Webb's answer but simply went on. "Because it's so different from my work. These four musicians are going to choose a tune in a few minutes, and despite them all knowing and having played it many times, they won't know what they're going to do until they do it. Improvisation. I love it, but I can't afford it. I have to know every move I'm going to make in advance. These guys," he waved his hand at the bandstand, "are spontaneous. It's exhilarating. Don't you agree?"

Webb considered. "Yes, I suppose it can be." Before Webb could say more, the lights dimmed and a voice from the sound system filled the room. "Ladies and gentlemen, the Blue Note is proud to present, in his first New York appearance, Tyler Browne and his quartet."

The saxophonist snapped his fingers several times and then the piano, bass and drums were playing, all lost in their own little world. The saxophonist listened for a while then put the horn to his lips and joined them in some song that Webb didn't recognize at all.

Webb watched Pearson. A slight smile creased his lips, and his head nodded in time to the band, his hand lightly tapping on the table. Webb looked at his watch. He wanted to get back to his hotel and forget Pearson now, distance himself from this place, this music, but now, it was too late. He'd have to wait for intermission.

They played for nearly an hour before the saxophonist thanked the audience to enthusiastic applause, and their sound was replaced by taped music. People were paying checks, getting up and starting to leave before the next set.

"Amazing," Pearson said. "He's a real talent." He turned to look at Webb. "What do you think?"

Webb was at a loss. He admitted one slow ballad had been nice, but for the most part, he just didn't get it. "Well, it was, ah, very lively."

Pearson smiled. "Lively. Yes, I like that." He sipped his coffee that the waitress had brought them during the music. She had slipped in so quietly that Webb had hardly noticed.

"Well, ah, the check is taken care of," Webb said. "And I really must get along." He got to his feet and stuck out his pudgy hand. "Good to see you again, Pearson. We'll have a money transfer on deposit as usual."

"You'd better," Pearson said, his eyes boring into Webb's. "Oh, by the way, how's the writing going? A detective novel, isn't it?"

Webb sat down again. He didn't remember telling Pearson about it. He couldn't lie to Pearson. "Not well. It's so hard to find a publisher or an agent." He tried to avoid Pearson's eyes.

"Rejected you, huh?"

Webb shrugged. "Resoundingly. They said it was derivative." The two editors he had tried to talk to today had blown him off, too. It was hopeless.

"Maybe it was," Pearson said. "It's a tough game. There are lots of P.I. books out there." He looked at Webb then said, "Write something different."

"Different?" Webb couldn't imagine anything more different than his transvestite hero.

"Yeah," Pearson said. "You know the old saw. Write what you know. Write about yourself; what you do besides your teaching job." Pearson continued to look at him. "Our business," he said.

Webb stared back for a moment, light emerging in his mind. Of course. What did he really know about sex change operations or how long they took? He'd have to know more, learn about jazz, all the details, but he knew a lot already. Pearson nodded at him, seeing that he understood.

"Think about it," Pearson said. "You already know the ending."

"Yes," Webb said, getting to his feet again. He started to walk away then turned back.

Pearson looked at him. "Was there something else?"

"No, no, I was just wondering."

"Yes?"

"Will you see the play first? I can arrange a ticket."

Pearson thought for a moment and smiled. "Maybe. I'll let you know. I always liked Neil Simon."

"I can't believe you got tickets to this show, Arthur, and such great seats. I'm so glad you had me join you."

Webb smiled at her. "Oh, I have a few contacts." He had the program open, studying the cast list, wondering if...

"Ladies and gentlemen, due to serious illness, the part of Clarissa will be played by her understudy for this performance. Thank you for your patience and understanding."

"Oh, no," Janet said. "I wonder what happened to her."

Webb smiled and leaned back in his seat as the curtain opened.

"Matinee," *Death Dines In*. Edited by Claudia Bishop & Dean James. 2004. Berkley Publishing Group.

CHILD'S PLAY

Wilson Childs stood as always: flat-footed, eyes shut, tenor saxophone held straight out in front of him, left foot barely tapping out the tempo. He blew the first two notes of "Stella By Starlight" and let them hang in the air, waiting for the answering chord from the pianist, then frowned as he realized the drummer had missed his count. He gave an inward sigh, and without looking back, he could feel the whole rhythm section scuffling to find the groove, glancing at each other with questioning looks—was it me? —trying to settle in before eight bars had gone by.

Wilson looked out over the crowd. Even the few people paying attention didn't know anything was wrong. The rest continued their conversations and laughter over the din of blenders, coffee machines and drink orders shouted by jeans clad waitresses, who were probably students at Berkeley. It never changed, Wilson Childs thought, except now the club was smoke-free.

They were in yet another reincarnation of the Jazz Workshop on Broadway, nestled in the North Beach mix of sex shops, titty bars, Italian bakeries and coffee shops, just a short walk from Columbus Avenue and City Lights Bookstore.

Wilson played with the melody, turning it inside out, waiting for a sign that somebody knew where one was. Finally, Dean James, the youngish pianist, laid down the chords, and everybody found it and settled down. Wilson decided to give it to Dean for his show of taking charge first. He nodded toward him and took the horn out of his mouth. He gave the drummer a look, but he was paying attention to the music now and not the blonde in the short skirt, her long legs crossed, gazing at him from her perch on a high stool at the bar.

Wilson folded his hands across the horn and sighed again, remembering another time at the Jazz Workshop, years ago, when the whole place was blue with smoke and the bar was crowded with musicians catching Wilson Childs and Quincy Simmons on an off Monday night. Miles had been there too, Wilson remembered, talking to some guy at the bar, getting ready for his opening at the Blackhawk, and Wilson knew, scouting him. Wilson was the hot young tenor player then. Big things were expected of him, but now they were gone, as surely as Quincy Simmons was gone.

The word was on the street. Coltrane had left Miles to form his own group, and Miles was looking for a replacement. Wilson caught Miles glancing at him once and smiled as Quincy Simmons spun out three choruses on the Monk tune, "Well You Needn't." During the bass solo, Miles passed the bandstand and in that gravely voice said, "Hey, Childs, I'll call you."

But Miles had not called, not that night, not ever, after what happened later that night.

Now, Wilson tipped his head to the left, listening to Dean's last sixteen bars, put the horn back in his mouth, playing like, *oh shit, give me this thing,* turning Stella into a whore. He played four choruses that made the whole band shake their heads, and then took it out. The rest of the set went okay and was acknowledged by a few real listeners. Wilson set his horn down and made for the tiny band room in back, except for Dean, who he tapped on the shoulder, Wilson ignored the rhythm section.

He stepped out the back door into the little alleyway and lit a cigarette, thinking again about Quincy Simmons, wondering what had happened to him. Was he really dead? He'd seen the notice in a small jazz magazine—what was it ten years ago— but he'd never believed it. He let his mind drift back to that earlier night at the Workshop in 1961.

The band was smoking, and Wilson was sorry that Miles had left early. Wilson and Quincy had left in Quincy's car, headed for Bop City, see who was around, maybe play a little, when the cops pulled them over.

"Oh shit," Wilson said, tapping the baggy of grass in his coat pocket. "I can't handle this."

"Put it under the seat, man," Quincy said, checking the rear-view mirror. "It's probably nothing."

But it wasn't nothing. The cops eyed the saxophone case, got them both out of the car and searched the vehicle. The cop found the baggy under the front seat and held it up happily. "Well, well," he said, glancing at Wilson. "Whatta we have here?"

The cop was young, younger than Wilson, but white, and this was San Francisco. He stood by, his hand resting on his gun, seemingly uneasy about the whole thing.

"This yours?" the young cop asked Wilson.

Wilson sighed. He didn't need a bust, not now, not with his record. But before he could answer, Quincy cut in, "It's mine," he said. "Just holding for a friend."

Wilson looked at Quincy, tried to tell him to shut up with his eyes, but Quincy wouldn't stop. "He's got nothing to do with it, Officer. He didn't even know I had it."

"Sure," the cop said. "Am I going to find anything else?" He stepped back and put his hand on his gun.

Quincy sighed. "Yes. Under the driver's seat."

The young cop looked from Quincy to Wilson and made a quick decision. "Cuff him," he told his partner, who bent Quincy over the hood of the car and locked the cuffs on his wrists.

His eyes on Wilson, the cop reached under the seat, felt around and came up with a gun. "Well, well," he said, smiling. He held it up for his partner and Wilson to see. "Looks like I did have probable cause, huh?"

Wilson didn't have to act surprised. He just stood, frozen, and said nothing. It was a small gun, one of those short-barrel kind he'd seen in movies hundreds of times.

"You drive?" the young cop asked, turning his attention back to Wilson. Wilson nodded. "License?" Wilson took out his wallet and showed the cop. He studied it for a moment and handed it back. "Okay, because I'm a nice guy, I'm going to give you a break. You can drive your partner's car home. I'm not going to find anything else in the car, am I?"

"No," Wilson said, his eyes moving quickly to Quincy, who was already in the police car, staring at Wilson. "Can I talk to him for a minute? I need to ask him who he wants me to call."

"Yeah, go ahead." He nodded for his partner to open the door. While they conferred, Wilson leaned in to Quincy.

"Man, what the fuck you doing with a gun? Why you want to do this?"

Quincy smiled. "No big thing, man. You don't need a bust now. Next week you'll be with Miles. Just get me out, okay?"

"Okay, let's go," the young cop said, brushing Wilson back and shutting the door of the police car.

"I got it covered," Wilson said to Quincy. "Don't worry."

Then Wilson Childs stood on the curb, watching the police car drive away.

But it didn't go the way they thought. Quincy Simmons' previous record was brought up, and an overzealous D.A. decided to apply the screws; Quincy was remanded to county jail, bail pending, while the gun was checked out. He faced maybe a year if they pushed it. However, the gun was traced to a convenience store robbery, and Quincy had more to explain than he ever could.

Wilson visited him once, sitting across from him,

separated by the thick glass, talking on the phones. "You okay, man?" Wilson said, sickened to see Quincy in the jailhouse jumpsuit. Wilson knew what it was like. He'd been there himself.

"Yeah. P.D. says they'll give me a week to get my shit together after the arraignment, but I might be looking at a year, six months if I'm lucky."

Wilson closed his eyes and gripped the phone. "Look, man, I can tell them it was—"

Quincy cut him off. "No, you wait for that call from Miles. Just do the gig. You don't need this shit now, you hear me?"

Wilson nodded, knowing he should ignore Quincy, step up and let them know they had the wrong man, but he didn't. There was nothing he could do about the gun. Quincy did manage a release but never turned up for sentencing.

Wilson never saw him again. He was just gone, disappeared, dropped off and out of sight.

The rumors flowed, but nobody knew for sure, and Wilson lived with it every day of his life for the past twenty years, haunted by his own failure. Some years later, a story turned up in one of the jazz magazines that Quincy Simmons had died, but Wilson didn't believe it. He just couldn't.

Wilson put out his cigarette and started back inside when he ran into Dean. "Oh, there you are," Dean said. "Did you hear? Some guy at the bar told me."

"Hear what?"

"Quincy Simmons. They found him."

* * *

Wilson played through the rest of the night in a fog, just going through the motions. He couldn't keep his mind off Quincy Simmons. Found, just like that, after all this time. He'd grilled Dean but the young pianist didn't know the details, just that Quincy had been found playing piano in a gospel mission in Los Angeles, a refuge for homeless men, a place to feed their spirit and their bodies.

"It was in the paper today, I guess," Dean had said.

Wilson wanted to see for himself. He packed up his horn and walked down Columbus Avenue to an all-night coffee shop and bought a paper out of the machine. Inside, he took a booth, ordered coffee and a sandwich, and scanned through the *Los Angeles Times*. The story was in the back pages, sandwiched between a bunch of ads. Wilson folded the paper and read and reread the story several times.

Lost Jazzman Found

Quincy Simmons, once prominent on the jazz scene, was recently discovered at a homeless shelter and church, playing piano and living in a small room in back of the shelter. Simmons disappeared almost twenty-five years ago following an arrest for drug possession and an illegal hand gun. Simmons was released on bail, but when it was thought the gun had been used in a convenience store robbery, his bail had been revoked pending further investigation.

Simmons had jumped bail and was never seen again, until now. At the time of his arrest, he was appearing with saxophonist Wilson Childs at the Jazz Workshop in San Francisco. Sources say Simmons has little memory of the arrest and subsequent flight, or how he got back to playing piano again.

"Oh, Quincy," Wilson said to himself. "You never knew, and nobody could find you."

"More coffee?"

Wilson looked up at the waitress. "What? Oh yes, thank you."

"Something wrong with the sandwich?" she asked, looking at his untouched plate.

"No, guess I just wasn't as hungry as I thought," Wilson said. He picked up the sandwich, took a small bite and nodded at the waitress. She shrugged and walked away.

Wilson looked at the article again. There was no writer listed, just *Times* staff writer. He grabbed his horn and the check and went up front to pay, getting a handful of quarters back from the cashier. He found a pay phone and dialed information for the *Los Angeles Times.*

"City Desk," a gruff voice said.

"Hello," Wilson said, not quite sure what to ask. "I'm calling about a story you ran today, Quincy Simmons, the piano player."

"Who?" The man sounded annoyed.

"Quincy Simmons. The story was on page twenty-seven. It says, 'Lost Jazzman Found.'"

"Hang on," the voice said.

Wilson could hear paper rattled and shuffled.

"Yeah, I got it. What about it?"

"Can you tell me who wrote it? It just says staff writer. I need to talk to the writer. It's important."

"Hang on," the voice said again. "Let me check the assignment sheet."

Wilson waited, desperate for a cigarette.

"Okay, here it is. Anne Carson, but she won't be in till in the morning, and no I can't give you her home number. Call back then."

"Thanks," Wilson said, but the voice was already gone.

Wilson waited till nine the next morning to call. He was switched around several times, then finally he heard, "Anne Carson."

"Hello," Wilson said. He'd rehearsed what he was going to say, but now his mind went blank. "This is Wilson Childs. I..."

"Oh my God," Carson said. "I was just pulling your bio. Are you in L.A.?"

'No, but I wanted to talk to you about the story you wrote."

"I'm doing a follow-up, or will, if I can convince my editor." She sounded excited, urgent.

"Did you see Quincy? Is he...is he okay? I need to talk to him."

"Physically, yes, but he's pretty foggy on things. It's like he's missing twenty-five years or something. He seemed nervous talking to me."

"He never knew," Wilson said.

"Never knew what?"

"The gun charge, about it being dropped. That's why he jumped bail."

"Oh Jesus," Carson said. "Jesus." There was a long pause while they both listened to their thoughts.

"Look, Mr. Wilson, I know this is a dumb thing to say, but I've been a fan of yours for a long time. I have some of your records, I even found one you made with Quincy Simmons, 'Childs Play.' Do you remember it?"

Wilson smiled. "Yes." He was not surprised at the question. He'd recorded a lot, and sometimes the sessions got mixed up in his mind like with a lot of musicians.

"Oh, it was wonderful, well still is," Carson said. "Look, can you come to L.A.? I could meet you, take you to see Quincy and—"

Wilson cut her off. "Don't tell him I'm coming. I want to be the one to tell him, okay?"

"Sure," Carson said, "I understand."

Wilson knew she didn't but was grateful to her for saying so. "I have one more night here. I can come down Sunday morning."

"Great!" Carson said. "I'll meet you. Let me know the flight time and airline."

"I will. Miss Carson?"

"Yes?"

"Thank you."

Wilson walked out of baggage claim at LAX, carrying a small bag and his horn. He stopped, looked around and saw a young blonde woman leaning on a Honda, waving at him and arguing with a security guard.

Wilson walked over. "Miss Carson?"

"Yes," she said, putting out her hand. She was maybe thirty, Wilson thought, the same age as his daughter, dressed in jeans, a sweater and running shoes. "It's a pleasure."

Wilson put his bag and horn in the backseat and got in the car. Carson started the engine and pulled away while punching in numbers on a cell phone. "You're early enough for the service," she said, glancing at Wilson.

He noticed the ashtray, the pack of cigarettes on the dashboard. "Do you mind?" he said. He pulled out his own from the leather jacket pocket.

Carson nodded and spoke into the phone. "Reverend Stiles?...Anne Carson. He's here, in my car...Uh huh, uh huh. Just tell Quincy he's going to have a visitor...Okay, see ya then." She closed the phone, cut off two cars and turned down Lincoln Boulevard, heading for the Santa Monica Freeway, Wilson guessed.

She cracked both windows as they lit cigarettes and relaxed a little, smiling at Wilson. "So, you haven't seen Quincy since..."

"I visited him in jail, but no, not since then."

Carson nodded. "He looks almost the same, well hell, so do you," she said, smiling at him. "It's just so...so weird. How does a guy like that just disappear for so long?"

"How did you find him?" Wilson asked.

"I didn't," she said. "Reverend Stiles—he runs the mission—called me. I'd done a story on the shelter, and he knew I was a jazz fan. Quincy mentioned something about playing piano with you once, so I went down to check it out, and whoa. There he was. Quincy Simmons, playing hymns and gospel songs for a bunch of guys who were just waiting for a hot meal. I couldn't believe it."

The Sunday morning traffic was light, and they made good time. The radio was on low and tuned to a jazz station. Wilson shook his head, remembering Miles at the Blackhawk, and wondered how close he'd come to being on that record.

Carson took the Harbor Freeway to downtown and exited on 6th Street. Wilson hadn't been to L.A. in a long time, but he remembered the area. They drove down 6th, past boarded up storefronts, liquor stores and men standing on corners or stretched out sleeping in doorways. Carson turned off 6th and pulled up in front of a building with a sign that read, "All Souls Mission & Church. All Are Welcome Here."

They got out of the car. "Let's put your bag and horn in the trunk," Carson said. She unlocked the trunk, and Wilson put his bag in. "I'll take the horn with me," he said.

Carson smiled at him. "I hoped you'd say that." She stuffed a camera in her shoulder bag and led Wilson inside.

Reverend Stiles, a small, wiry black man in rimless glasses, was at the pulpit reading from the Bible as they slipped in and sat down in the back row. He finished the passage, closed the Bible and addressed the audience of shabbily dressed men of all ages. Wilson suddenly felt uncomfortable, then he saw Quincy, rising from a chair and seating himself at an old upright piano.

"And now with Brother Quincy's fine help, we'll all sing and then have ourselves a hot breakfast. Praise the Lord."

The men murmured along as Quincy played the chords for some old gospel tune Wilson vaguely remembered but played somehow differently by Quincy, who made it almost a blues.

Wilson listened for a minute and then unzipped his bag, put his horn together and walked up the aisle next to the wall. He watched Quincy, head down, his hands outstretched on the keyboard, oblivious to the voices of the reluctant men singing behind him.

Wilson waited for the next chorus and then began to play as he walked closer to the piano. Quincy's head jerked up, and he looked around, and for a moment, their eyes locked. Wilson watched recognition wash over Quincy's face, saw a slight smile forming as Wilson reached the piano. He played a line, repeated it, and Quincy fell right in, as if twenty-five years was only yesterday.

Wilson looked out over the audience as he and Quincy segued into a more modern blues, their own kind of gospel. Quincy was smiling now, feeding Wilson chords, comping behind him like they were back in the Jazz Workshop.

Wilson played two more choruses and then took it out. As the men filed out to the dining room, he put his horn on top of the piano. Quincy stood up and came toward him. They looked at each other for a long moment and then hugged. Wilson held

Quincy by the shoulders. "I missed you, man," he said. "Where the hell you been?"

"Oh, around," Quincy said. "I'm not so sure about all of it, but I'm glad to see you. Yes, I am."

Reverend Stiles and Anne Carson looked on. She snapped a couple of pictures and then finally Stiles said, "We have a nice breakfast, if you two gentlemen would like to join us."

In the dining room, on rough wooden tables and benches, Wilson and Quincy talked over ham slices and eggs. "How long you been here?" Wilson asked.

Quincy shrugged. "Oh, about six months, I guess. Before that it's all kind of hazy. All over, you know. I just lost track, lost myself I guess. Then I walked in here one afternoon, saw that piano and everything sort of came back." He sighed and looked away, nodded to Reverend Stiles and Anne Carson, who sat nearby, stealing glances at them. "I just couldn't make that jail scene, man. I just had to get away."

"Can we smoke in here?" Wilson held up his cigarettes to Reverend Stiles, who nodded yes. Wilson got one going and looked at Quincy. "Look, man, there's something I have to tell you."

Quincy looked at him. "What?"

"The gun charge was dropped, man. All you would have done is served time. It was dropped." Wilson took a deep drag on his cigarette and watched Quincy, saw the realization in his eyes.

"I tried to find you, man, I really did, but you were gone."

Quincy nodded. "And you put up the bail didn't you, got stuck when I took off?"

"Oh, that was nothing, man," Wilson said. "Forget it." He studied Quincy. "You know about ten years ago, *DownBeat* said you were dead."

"Yeah, I know," Quincy smiled. "That lady from the newspaper told me." He smiled again. "Guess it was just as well. People stopped lookin' for me then, huh?"

"I never believed it," Wilson said. "Quincy Simmons dead? No way."

"Hey," Quincy said, "did Miles ever call you?"

"Naw, he got Hank Mobley for the Blackhawk gig, and then Wayne Shorter after that. You ain't heard the shit he's playing now."

"Don't know if I want to," Quincy said. "I haven't heard much music lately. Tell me about you, man. You doing all right?"

Wilson shrugged. "I went with Basie for a while then all that fusion rock shit hit. Now we're in style again. There's a young cat, Wynton Marsalis, trumpet player, got famous and so did jazz again. Bunch of young bloods. They call them the young lions." Wilson shrugged and grinned. "I'm too old to be a young lion and not old enough to be an old veteran. Record companies tell me, 'Wilson Childs, you play good, but we can't market you.' Ain't that a bitch. But everybody is playing bebop again, and that's something I know how to do."

They talked for a long time. Telling stories, remembering the good times, and finally reached that point old friends do who have been apart for a long time. Reunited, caught up on things and the future looming in front of them. But the big question still hadn't been answered. Wilson suddenly realized that Quincy might as well have been in prison all this time.

"Can you talk about it, man?" Wilson asked, looking into Quincy's eyes. "What happened?"

Quincy held up his hands. "I don't know. A lot of it's hazy, but it was starting before I took off. I know we were doing well, but I couldn't shake feeling, lost, depressed. I don't know what you'd call it. That's why I bought the gun. I kept thinking somebody was coming after me. Sounds crazy, but I guess I was a little crazy.

"I saw this doctor for a while. He gave me these pills, supposed to make me feel better, but, I don't know, just seemed to make it worse. That's why I was hoping Miles would take you on. I just wanted to quit playing, go away for a while, but I knew you'd never let me do that."

Wilson shook his head, knowing Quincy was right, but also knowing Quincy would never have let him turn Miles down if he'd called.

"I just kind of drifted," Quincy continued. "For a while it was nice, not having the pressure, worrying about gigs, how I was playing, where the money was going to come from." He looked up at Wilson. "You understand what I'm saying?"

Wilson nodded. He knew. You choose this life, all those things Quincy said came with it. Only, you don't choose the life. It chooses you. But the rest of it, he could only imagine. Years of nothing but odd jobs, living hand to mouth, nobody knowing who you were or where you were, maybe not even knowing yourself.

"What about now? Whatever you want to do, I'll help you." Wilson grinned at him. "You're going to be famous now, you know, now that you're found again. I'm going to have to hit on you for a gig." Wilson studied him. "Do you want to play again? I heard you out there, man." He nodded toward the church. "It's still there."

Quincy nodded. "Reverend Stiles has been letting me practice, but until you walked in today, I wasn't sure."

Wilson grinned. "Well, motherfucker, let's go on the road then."

DownBeat picked up the story, courtesy of Anne Carson's follow-up profile in the *Times*, and then the phone never stopped ringing. The following month, Quincy Simmons and Wilson Childs were on the cover of three jazz magazines, and Anne had written the stories. Several record companies, including the one that had told Wilson they couldn't market him, were interested. Now it seemed they could.

A month later, a reunion gig was arranged at the Jazz Bakery in Los Angeles that sold out a week in advance. When they took the stand to an ovation and opened with one of the bop tunes they'd played years ago, Wilson could feel the adrenaline rush as Quincy's rich chords, like a lush carpet that makes you want to walk barefoot, filled the room. Wilson felt a great weight lifted from his shoulders as he walked to the microphone.

It was Wilson Childs who played better than ever.

"Child's Play," *Murder...and All That Jazz.* Edited by Robert J. Randisi. 2004. Signet.

"Child's Play," *The Jazz Fiction Anthology.* Edited by Sascha Feinstein & David Rife. 2009. Indiana University Press.

REHEARSAL

"I hate these things," Old Folks says as he unpacks the electric bass guitar. I watch him perform the electronic ritual, admiring his unhurried movements done with surprising grace for a man his size. His arms stretch the thin fabric of his T-shirt as he snaps the cord into the amplifier and adjusts the volume.

Old Folks would be more at home stroking two hundred years of German wood, walking in rich dark tones, but Ozzie's jazz, if it can still be called that, lends itself to the Fender bass.

In the harsh glare of the stage light, Old Folks' shaven head is dark and smooth, like polished mahogany. His eyes reflect the fatigue that comes with surviving thousands of one-nighters with Count Basie, Duke Ellington, and even a brief stint with Miles Davis. Old Folks was there once, like a footnote in a chapter of jazz history. But he's tired now and must, according to Ozzie, be disposed of.

His real name is David Lee Burroughs, but no one remembers that now. He was dubbed Old Folks—by me, I suddenly remember—after the song, and because he's more than twice the age of any of us, Ozzie included. He takes the kidding about his name good naturedly, but I wonder how he will react to Ozzie's plan.

There are disturbing rumors about Old Folks,

that he once served a year in jail for assault, but no one has asked about them or wants them confirmed. His gentle manner seems to belie such a reality. But Emerson Barnes, Ozzie's manager, claims they are true.

"Nearly killed a man," Emerson said, but Emerson is prone to exaggeration. I think telling us was for effect, to keep Brian and me on edge, but the possibility looms heavily on my mind as I wonder if Old Folks suspects he will not play a single note on this opening night.

The scenario is complex, and sadly, I'm to play a small role in its denouement. Despite his credits, Old Folks has not worked out. Not since a San Francisco concert when Ozzie nearly destroyed the dressing room in frustration over Old Folks failure to measure up to his expectations.

Two weeks' notice is the way it usually goes, but even though he's a major rising star, Ozzie is too insecure to confront Old Folks directly and honestly. Bowing to his wife's demands—"A friend of a friend just happens to need work," she said— Ozzie has instead chosen to humiliate the aging bassist and cover up his own mistake.

I light a cigarette and watch the bartender stack glasses in a metal rack. The empty seats and booths seem to mock us. I'm anxious for this farce to be over, but even for this, Ozzie is late. My impatience is transmitted to the drumsticks as I tap out idle rhythms on a cymbal. We all know our lines, the stage directions have been decided on, but everyone seems reluctant for the play to begin.

Someone has left the door open to the showroom

lounge. Heavy black drapes, pulled nearly across the entrance, muffle the sounds of bells, groans, delighted cries and the drone of a hundred conversations filtering in from the casino. Tonight, a maître d' will guard the entrance like a sentinel and admit the chosen few who have reservations. But now, except for the stage lights, the lounge is dark and deserted.

Old Folks and I sit alone on the stage waiting for Ozzie and Brian to arrive and put truth to the sign at the entrance that reads, "Rehearsal in Progress." So far there is none.

From behind the drums, I can see a pit boss roaming restlessly among the crap tables. A woman with flowing blonde hair and a paper cup of coins pauses at the entrance, glances in, then walks on impatiently.

It's cold outside and more snow threatens. This I know from an early morning tramp through the woods. But here, inside the hotel-casino without windows or clocks, I feel trapped, like a time traveler caught in a void. I wonder now why I have agreed to be a part of this. There is still time to back out, I tell myself. Confess and let Old Folks make a dignified departure.

"Where's the man?" Old Folks asks. He's settled on a bar stool and runs mammoth hands over the strings of the bass that's cradled across his lap like a shotgun. His eyes flick from the entrance to me.

"You know, Ozzie," I say carefully, avoiding his eyes, sure that my own will betray the knowledge of the scene about to unfold. Somehow I know he senses what is coming. He grunts in response and scans the music on the stand before him.

It's a difficult arrangement, Ozzie's new opening number, finished by Brian only two days ago. It too will play a part in the farce, designed as it is to unmask and degrade Old Folks. No one disputes his musical abilities, but sight reading is a long forgotten skill, and his failing is the wedge Ozzie will use to drive Old Folks away.

What of my own complicity in this plot? Old Folks deserves more than this sham Ozzie has planned. But I have agreed. Why? Is this what I wanted from music? Suddenly, I want to be out in the snow again, feel the crisp clear air on my face and gaze across the expanse of Lake Tahoe. But I'm too late. We both look up as the drapes are thrust aside.

Emerson Barnes strides in trailed by Brian, and finally, Ozzie himself. He wears a ski jacket and dark glasses, as if his escape can be made through the snow.

"All right, fellas, let's do it." Emerson Barnes smiles with confidence of a prosecuting attorney whose case is in the bag.

Brian takes his place at the piano, but for a moment he doesn't seem to know what to do. He is paler than usual, and I can see beads of sweat on his forehead. He thumbs through the music and strikes the keys, then finally pulls out the new arrangement as if he has just discovered it.

I don't envy Brian his role, but he has made his choice. He likes being a conductor. Bending to Emerson's insistence and Ozzie's promises, it is Brian who will actually break the news to Old

Folks. That's how we agreed it would go.

"Let's try the new opener," Brian says casually. He tries to catch my eye but I look away. I won't help him. Brian has made his choice and I've made mine. I suddenly want Old Folks to succeed, but as Brian counts us in, Old Folks is already in trouble, scuffling with the fast tempo, the notes that can only be a blur before his eyes.

Ozzie sneers in my direction, as if I'm responsible. Maybe I too will be gone before the night is over.

Brian stops us. "Can we try that again? Watch the key change at letter A," he says. He never looks at Old Folks. Brian is an excellent musician but he lacks moral strength. I wonder why I haven't noticed before. It is fear and ambition, I realize, that drives him.

We start and again, Old Folks stumbles. Impulsively, I make a deliberate mistake but regret it at once. I'm only prolonging the agony. I'm rewarded by a glance I take to mean surprised gratitude. Ozzie glares at me. Emerson turns away for a moment. This is not in the script. I'm holding up the proceedings.

"Sorry," I say, raising my hand.

We start for the third time. Ozzie joins us after the first eight bars, and miraculously, Old Folks is right on the money. Shaken, it is now Ozzie who stumbles over a phrase. He tries to press on but then drops out, letting the microphone dangle at his side.

"Come on, man, that's not it," Ozzie says. Old Folks seems to know what I want to tell him. If he could see behind Ozzie's dark glasses, he would find fear.

"What's the problem?" The hint of a smile crosses his face.

"The problem is, you played a wrong note." Ozzie stares at Old Folks defiantly.

Old Folks now grins openly. He knows Ozzie is bluffing. "Which one?"

Ozzie is a gifted singer, blessed with a booming voice, but he knows little about music. He turns to Emerson for help.

"Maybe the tempo is wrong," Emerson suggests. He nods to Brian, who sits rock still at the piano, staring at the keyboard as if the answer lies somewhere there.

We try again, and this time, Ozzie is taking no chances. He doesn't even bother with his entrance. "No, no, no," he says. He drops the microphone on the floor, jumps off the stage and starts for the exit. On cue, Emerson rises and follows. At the door, the two briefly confer in a halfhearted manner that fools no one, certainly not Old Folks, who stares into the darkness.

Ozzie then disappears through the drapes. Shrugging and shaking his head, Emerson returns. "Man's under a lot of pressure," he mumbles, just loud enough for us to hear. He calls Brian aside, who seems terrified now that the moment is at hand.

Old Folks looks at me. "What is this all about?"

I can do no more than shrug and feign a sudden interest in the height of one of my cymbals.

After an appropriate amount of time, Emerson

pushes Brian forward. He looks to me for support, but I only stare back impassively, fearing for Brian, but resolved to go no further. I know I will pay for it later.

"Ah, look," Brian begins. "Ozzie is a little upset. He says he can't..." His voice trails off under Old Folks' baleful stare.

Rising from the stool, Old Folks towers over Brian. "Ozzie can't what?"

My eyes dart to the open bass case on the floor beside him. I realize I'm looking to see if there's a weapon inside.

"I'm sorry," Brian stammers. "Ozzie says he can't open with you." Mission accomplished, Brian retreats behind the piano.

Old Folks sits down slowly and bows his head. His shoulders slump. He nods, and for the moment, there are only the filtered, distant sounds of the casino and glasses clinking as the bartender, oblivious to the little drama being played out, continues to work. Finally, Old Folks turns toward me. "Well, I guess we knew this was coming, didn't we?"

I have no answer, but his smile makes me uneasy. The stories about Old Folks flood through my mind. I only sit dumbly and wonder how I allowed myself to be part of this, sick inside with the knowledge that the new bass player, flown up from Los Angeles this morning, is now standing by in his room, awaiting word from Emerson to join the rehearsal.

Emerson stands rigidly, steeling himself for Old Folks' reaction, but it is nothing more than to pack up his bass, quietly shut the case and step down from the stage. Emerson moves aside for him to pass, but not before he slips an envelope into the big man's hand.

Old Folks never breaks stride until he reaches the heavy black drapes at the entrance. He stops then and looks back. I'm sure it is me he gazes at, then he is gone, lost in the casino crowd. The rest of us know Ozzie is by now securely locked in his room and won't appear until the first show.

Brian's sigh of relief is audible. He starts to speak, but Emerson cuts him off. "I'll call John," he says. "You can run down the show with him."

I get up and walk off the stage. "Where are you going?" Emerson demands.

"Out. Upstairs. I've had enough rehearsal for one day."

"Man, you still don't know what's happening, do you?" Emerson's voice is full of contempt, but I don't care now. I'm already thrusting the drapes aside, pushing through the throng of gamblers toward the elevators.

On my floor, there's a cart in front of Old Folks door. Inside, a maid is pulling sheets and blankets off the bed. She barely glances at me. "You lookin' for that big fella? He's already gone."

I nod and race back to the elevators. I stab at the down button, but when the doors open, Old Folks is waiting. The bass and a battered suitcase look like toys in his massive hands. My first impulse is to back out, but the doors have already closed behind me.

"I saw you goin' up," Old Folks says. He presses

the down button and stares at me impassively. "They got somebody else already lined up, right?"

I avert my eyes and nod, admitting my own guilt, hoping it will absolve me of my sins for knowing about the plan and not telling.

Old Folks grins suddenly. "One thing, man," he says. "I won't forget this."

I stand silently, taking in his words, feeling reprieved but not understanding. Does he plan revenge on Ozzie, or has he simply sensed my discomfort, understood my motives?

When we reach the lobby, he steps around two couples talking loudly about dinner plans. Old Folks turns and smiles at me, then disappears into the crowd. The couples look at me questioningly.

"It's all right," I say. "I'm going up."

"Rehearsal," *The River Underground: An Anthology of Nevada Fiction.* Edited by Shaun T. Griffin. 2001. University of Nevada Press.

AMBROSE, WILL YOU PLEASE COOL IT!

Grover Dodds, known affectionately to his friends as Grover the Groover, leaned across the counter at the midtown drum shop and spoke in hushed tones, about to confess an unpardonable sin.

"I did a society gig, man," he whispered in a raspy voice he used when trying to imitate Miles Davis. Glancing around nervously for would be eavesdroppers, he peered at me from behind black-rimmed, dark sunglasses and thoughtfully fingered a pair of Regal Tip sticks that I'd left on the counter.

"It was a bad scene, man, I mean really like unbelievable."

I could well imagine. The fact that "the Groover" had done any gig was unbelievable.

Grover was the last of the hipster beboppers, at least in dress, talk and mannerisms. There the similarity ended. Grover spent most of his time in the drum shop, talking drums with anybody he could corner, but no one had so much as seen him on a practice pad, let alone on an actual gig. There were rumors that Grover once auditioned for Woody Herman, but most of us thought it was Grover who had created the rumor himself, and since Woody was no longer available to confirm or deny, Grover remained a legend in his own mind.

The proud owner of some ancient white pearl Slingerland drums, Grover claimed they were the legacy of the legendary Babe Dodds. But like the Woody Herman claim, most of us thought that too was a figment of Grover's fertile imagination. The only thing Grover shared with Baby was the same last name, and that was purely coincidental.

This and the fact that Grover had actively campaigned for Dizzy Gillespie's presidential run were Grover's only claims to fame. But Grover and a society band? That bordered on the supernatural. It was easy to visualize Rod Serling standing in the background.

"Meet Grover Dodds, itinerant jazz drummer, who stepped into a..."

"It was really weird, man," Grover went on. "And the leader, this Ambrose Agony cat, he was just too much."

"Ambrose Anthony," I corrected, trying to imagine this ill-fated meeting. Grover, the jive talking hipster, whose goal in life was to jam with Dizzy, and Ambrose Anthony, one of New York's top society band leaders, seemed as unlikely as Buddy Rich working with Lawrence Welk.

"Now you gotta be cool, man," Grover said. "I wouldn't want this to get around the street, you dig?"

I dug. My secrecy sworn, Grover the Groover told his tale.

* * *

"Well, man, the bread was a little short last week, so when I ran into this cat I know at the Musician's Union, he turned me on to Ambrose Agony, er, Anthony. Like he's a society leader—country clubs, weddings, bar mitzvahs, that kind of square stuff—but he sometimes uses jazz cats. I figure he can't be too square if he digs jazz, and hey, Bird did some gigs like that with Red Rodney. So, since nothin' else was happenin', I figure to give Ambrose a call and tell him, like I'm available.

"He's not in, but I do get this chick who says she's like his secretary. Man, I mean even Dizzy didn't have a secretary. Anyway, I rap with this chick, you know, tell her I got eyes to blow with Ambrose. She tells me I got to come in for an interview. I figure she meant an audition. You believe that, man? An interview for a gig, not an audition, an interview. So, I take my snare and some brushes and make it on down to the office. But, I'm really thinkin' more about the chick than the gig. I mean if she looks as good as she sounds, there are other possibilities if the gig don't turn out, you dig?

"Well, the office is in the penthouse over on Madison Avenue. So, I go on up, and there's this chick, sittin' there lookin' every bit as fine as she sounded on the phone. She tells me Ambrose is still not around, but I figure this is cool because I can rap with her until the cat shows. But nothin' man, no action at all, and I give it my best shot. Anyway, she says I should talk with Ambrose's assistant for the interview. And guess what. It is an interview, not an audition.

"Now, this cat is a real drag. He don't want me to play for him at all. He just asks me a lot of question about who I gigged with and do I have a tux. Man, I felt like I was trying to get a job. Anyway, I can tell this cat don't dig me at all even though I tell him I auditioned with Woody once. He keeps lookin' at my goatee real funny and asks me why I wear shades indoors. Like you know, just a general put-down. But he does take my number and says something might come up, so I split, figuring he's just coppin' out. I mean I was hip to him.

"By Saturday, I've forgotten the whole scene except for the chick. Then she calls me. She says I'm to be at a place called the River Club out on the Island for a special gig and that Ambrose would dig it if I came and blew a couple of tunes and would fifty beans be okay. Well, man, fifty beans is solid anytime, and since I'm not giggin' anywhere else, I give her a definite yes and also score a visit to her pad on Sunday.

"Well, when I arrive on the scene, I can see right away it's not going to be any Newport thing. I mean, there's Caddys and Lincolns parked all over and even a cat at the door takin' names. He got a little bugged with me and tells me I got to take my drums and go around back. I don't dig this, man. I mean I'm not a waiter, but what could I do? Ambrose is pickin' up the tab, right?

"So I go in and a couple of cats are there, but Ambrose is not, but I know I got the right place because I see this little sign on the piano that says:

Music by Ambrose Anthony
of New York.

"Now this really wigs me out. I mean can you imagine going down to the Village Vanguard and seeing a sign on the piano that says:

Music by Thelonious Monk
of New York.

"Anyway, I introduce myself to the cats, and one of the trumpet players says, 'Oh is Ambrose going to love you.' So, I figure Ambrose has heard me blow, so I set up my tubs and just dig the scene for a while.

"The place was filling up fast, and I mean these people were really dressed. The chicks were all in long gowns, and the cats were in tuxes, which made it hard to tell the musicians from the people. Very strange, man.

"Well, I'm just about to look for a taste and maybe rap with some of the chicks when this trumpet player says, 'Oh God, here comes Ambrose, and Harry isn't here yet.'

"Now it turns out Harry is Ambrose's regular drummer. When Ambrose finds out Harry isn't there, he like freaks out because it's time to blow. I mean he's running around yelling, 'Where's Harry, where's Harry? I'll kill him.' Well, man, there was no need for Ambrose to freak, 'cause I was, like, there, you dig? Then Ambrose spots me.

"'You, who are you?' he asks, pointing at me.

"So, like I tell him, I'm there to do the jazz tunes,

and I can blow for Harry till he shows. Well, Ambrose just looks kind of sick. I guess he was really worried about Harry, but he finally tells me to play, which is what I been trying to tell him. Weird cat, man.

"So, I sit down at the drums, and right away, I notice there are no charts. I mean a ten-piece band and they got no charts. Well, I figure these cats must really fake good. Ambrose just looks at us and says, 'Some Enchanted Evening,' and goes into his bag like, ah one, ah two, and we start playin'.

"I lay down some time on my K Zildian ride cymbal, and the band is playing, and I tell you, man, it is sad. Man, I never heard anything like that. There's like no chance to swing. They are into their own thing, and I don't know what that is. But even wilder is Ambrose. He's up there in front, wavin' and flappin' his arms like he's going to take off. Man, he is really conducting.

"Well, I'm watchin' him, and he's looking at me kind of funny. His face is getting all red, and I'm thinking 'Some Enchanted Evening' is pretty square for an opener, but Ambrose, man, he's lookin' at me hard now. I thought his eyes were going to pop out. But the other cats, they don't pay any attention to Ambrose. I guess they were used to seeing him like that, but for me, it was weird.

"He keeps watchin' me, and I figure maybe I should play louder, so I do, and add some figures on the snare like Shelly used to do with Kenton, and drop some bombs on the bass drum, but Ambrose don't dig it. He is really flipping out now, and he starts coming over to me, still flapping his arms and bouncing up and down and smiling at those chicks dancing by.

"He finally gets to me, and you know what he does then? He starts singing right in my ear. Now, like I was saying, we're playing 'Some Enchanted Evening,' right? And here is this weird cat, Ambrose, singing in my ear, only not the right words. Instead, he's singing:

> Lighter on the cymbal,
> Nothing on the bass drum
> Keep the music snappy
> Make the people happy.

"Well, man, that was just too much. I mean I've done some far out gigs, but this was the end, like this never happened. So, I tell him. I mean I know he's the leader and all, but I was bugged, man, you dig? So, I tell him, Ambrose will you please cool it!

"Ambrose looks like I slapped him, but he goes back in front of the band and starts to calm down a little, and he don't look at me for the rest of the night. So, I'm wondering, how long are we going to play 'Some Enchanted Evening?' I mean they just keep playing the melody, and then Ambrose yells, 'Lady is a Tramp,' and so help me, they go right into it without stopping. Same tempo and all, and like, that's the way it goes all night.

"Man, I felt like some kind of machine playing the same tempo for an hour at a time, but that's what we do. I keep looking and hoping Harry might show up, but he never does, so I'm like stuck for the whole gig. Ambrose wavin' his arms and the band getting juiced without Ambrose knowing about it—no booze on Ambrose gigs, and wavin' at all these old chicks dancing by saying, 'Oh, Mr. Anthony, the music is simply divine.' I mean it was a real crazy scene.

"Well, finally, it's over, and I'm really beat. I feel like I've been choppin' wood or something. And I'm so dragged. I just pack up my drums, and tell Ambrose, 'Later!'

"I split and go home and get stoned. I mean I just want to forget the whole thing. No more of those for me ever."

I had listened and knew what I'd heard, but I still couldn't believe it. "Grover, you don't mean Ambrose wanted you again?"

"Oh yeah, man. When they mailed the bread, there was a note saying they'd recommended me to Lester Lanin, and I hear he's even bigger than Ambrose."

ABOUT THE AUTHOR

Bill Moody lives in Northern California where he hosts a weekly jazz radio show and performs throughout the Bay Area with a variety of jazz groups. He is currently at work on his eighth Evan Horne jazz novel.

OTHER TITLES FROM DOWN AND OUT BOOKS

See www.DownAndOutBooks.com for complete list

By Anonymous-9
Bite Hard

By J.L. Abramo
Catching Water in a Net
Clutching at Straws
Counting to Infinity
Gravesend
Chasing Charlie Chan
Circling the Runway

By Trey R. Barker
2,000 Miles to Open Road
Exit Blood
Death is Not Forever
No Harder Prison (*)

By Richard Barre
The Innocents
Bearing Secrets
Christmas Stories
The Ghosts of Morning
Blackheart Highway
Burning Moon
Echo Bay
Lost

By Eric Beetner and
JB Kohl
Over Their Heads

By Eric Beetner and
Frank Scalise
The Backlist
The Shortlist (*)

By Rob Brunet
Stinking Rich

By Dana Cameron (editor)
Murder at the Beach:
Bouchercon Anthology 2014

By Stacey Cochran
Eddie & Sunny

By Mark Coggins
No Hard Feelings

By Tom Crowley
Vipers Tail
Murder in the Slaughterhouse

By Frank De Blase
Pine Box for a Pin-Up
Busted Valentines and Other
Dark Delights

By Les Edgerton
The Genuine, Imitation, Plastic
Kidnapping

By A.C. Frieden
Tranquility Denied
The Serpent's Game
The Pyongyang Option (*)

By Jack Getze
Big Numbers
Big Money
Big Mojo
Big Shoes

(*)—Coming Soon

OTHER TITLES FROM DOWN AND OUT BOOKS

See www.DownAndOutBooks.com for complete list

By Richard Godwin
Wrong Crowd

By William Hastings (editor)
*Stray Dogs: Writing from the
Other America*

By Matt Hilton
No Going Back
Rules of Honor
The Lawless Kind (*)

By Darrel James,
Linda O. Johnston &
Tammy Kaehler (editors)
Last Exit to Murder

By David Housewright &
Renée Valois
The Devil and the Diva

By David Housewright
Finders Keepers
Full House

By Jon & Ruth Jordan (editors)
*Murder and Mayhem in
Muskego*
Cooking with Crimespree

By Andrew McAleer &
Paul D. Marks (editors)
Coast to Coast

By Bill Moody
Czechmate

The Man in Red Square
Solo Hand
The Death of a Tenor Man
The Sound of the Trumpet
Bird Lives!
Mood Swings

By Gary Phillips
The Perpetrators
Scoundrels (Editor)
Treacherous

By Robert J. Randisi
Upon My Soul
Souls of the Dead
Envy the Dead (*)

By Ryan Sayles
The Subtle Art of Brutality
Warpath

By Anthony Neil Smith
Worm

By Liam Sweeny
Welcome Back, Jack

By Lono Waiwaiole
Wiley's Lament
Wiley's Shuffle
Wiley's Refrain
Dark Paradise

By Vincent Zandri
Moonlight Weeps

(*)—Coming Soon